Pauline B

Praise

Fortuna

"London's Little Italy i[s] ... conjures up passionate characters and tempestuous situations . . . Ferrari's strengths as a scriptwriter (she has worked on *EastEnders* and *Casualty*) show through in the taut, thrilling storylines . . .There is a depth of humanity and understanding in her heroines' impossible situations."

Eastern Daily Press

"These two books provide not only an important historical perspective for all Anglo-Italians, but also a pointer to those values we should seek to retain for the future. Highly recommended reading."

Luigi Sterlini, Backhill, Rivista Della Comunita Italiana

Fortunata

"A romantic novel with power and pace . . . Resonates with authenticity."

Morning Star

"An engrossing tale of personal commitment and ordinary everyday occurrences which any of us will recognise: love, death, jealousy, passion and regret."

Luigi Sterlini, Backhill, Rivista Della Comunita Italiana, 1993

Angelface

"Love and fear, duty and hope mingle in a magic mixture which makes the . . . novel . . . hard to put down."

Evening Echo

The Girl From Norfolk With The Flying Table

"It's one of those books where you snarl at anyone who interrupts you reading it – recommendations don't come much higher."

The Big Issue

"Here is a whiff of lost youth for all who breathed the heady air of the 1960's – but possibly did not inhale as deeply as they claim – during the exciting decade that ushered in a cultural revolution . . . This well paced and very readable novel . . . deals with the lives and would-be loves of a group of Beatles' fans . . . this is a story told with compassion and humour."

Eastern Daily Press

"Brings the era to joyful life through her headstrong female characters."

Yorkshire Evening Post

"An engaging portrait of an era."

Independent on Sunday

Joanna
and the
Weatherman

Joanna and the Weatherman

LILIE FERRARI

POOLBEG

Published 2002
by Poolbeg Press Ltd.
123 Grange Hill, Baldoyle,
Dublin 13, Ireland
Email: poolbeg@poolbeg.com

©Lilie Ferrari 2002

Copyright for typesetting, layout, design
© Poolbeg Group Services Ltd.

1 3 5 7 9 10 8 6 4 2

A catalogue record for this book is available from the British Library.

ISBN 1 84223 089 1

Cover Designed by Splash
Typeset by Patricia Hope in Goudy 11/14.5
Printed by Cox & Wyman

www.poolbeg.com

About the Author

Lilie Ferrari was, among other things, an unmarried mother in the sixties, a waitress in the South of France and a teacher in California before gaining a Master's Degree in French Literature. She then went on to work at the British Film Institute, where she worked in the Television Unit, taking a particular interest in popular dramas and soap operas. From there she went to the BBC, script-editing for *EastEnders*. Now a full-time television scriptwriter, she lives in Norfolk.

Acknowledgements

Somali buranbur poem by Mohamoud Osman
(Copyright untraceable)

Philip Larkin, *This Be the Verse*
Faber and Faber Ltd, 1974

'*First Love Never Dies*', words and music by
Bob Morris & Jimmy Seals.
©Copyright 1961 Golden West Melodies Incorporated & Four
Star Sales Company Incorporated, USA.
Acuff Rose Music Limited, 25 James Street, London W1.
Used by permission of Music Sales Ltd.
All Rights Reserved. International Copyright Secured.

Bart Simpson alarm clock quotes courtesy of
Wesco Limited and Twentieth Century Fox Limited

Scott Walker: A Deep Shade of Blue by Mike Watkinson
and Pete Anderson,
Virgin Books, 1994

'*Subterranean Homesick Blues*', written by Bob Dylan
Copyright Sony/ATV Music Publishing

'*Joanna*', written by Tony Hatch and Jackie Trent
Copyright Sony/ATV Music Publishing

For Jasmine

Chapter One

Young girls always talk a lot.
I have got a grievance against you girls.
If you don't lower your speech
Who will marry you, since we men are suspicious of you?

SOMALI BURANBUR POEM *by Mohamoud Osman (Haynwade).*

No no no. I don't want to go. I don't want to leave my dad and our flat and our life. I'm supposed to be meeting Oombe in the morning to go down the Africa Centre, meet some Somali boys just got here from the big Harerge camp in Ethiopia, word says they got good shirts they'll sell for almost nothing, selling their belongings to survive till Immigration chucks them out or they get their first dole money. I got plans, I got a life, it's all here, Tottenham, Mildmay Estate, life on the walkways and the stairwells, nights down the African Allstars, dancing and too much

1

khat, and the wide grin of Isaaq boys wanting to dance (and that's all they want to do), and me and Oombe shoplifting a bit in the WH Smith on the High Road, nothing big, some pens and a cookery book for Oombe's mum maybe – Delia Smith so she can imagine a life of roast dinners and blackberry and apple pies and three-leaf salads instead of rice and rice and rice.

It's my life, I don't want to leave it, but my mum's dragging me out, and the puppy's yelping and I'm hanging onto the door but she prises my fingers off and grips my wrist and twists like her hand's turned into a pair of pliers, and the last I see of my dad, he's red-faced and furious and telling us we're assholes and if we go we can't ever come back he'll change the locks, and the hysterical dog grabs the strap of my boot buckle in its teeth and won't let go, and I'm kicking it hard but it just yelps and hangs on, till Mum snatches it up and heaves us out of the door, slamming it hard, then stands there, heavy breathing.

Silence. Next door, I can see the net curtain by the Kapoors's kitchen sink twitch shut. She's got a kid on the draining board watching us. I can see its dark hair. Constant subject for scrutiny we are, says Mum. Usually says. But not now. Now she stands staring at the door, as if she can make it open again. I send her a brain message – *go back* – but she doesn't hear it, and with a little sharp breath she ushers me down the walkway towards the stairs, wriggling puppy under her arm, dragging my bin-bag full of the wrong clothes and her plastic launderette bag, the one she got free after working there for three weeks and not jacking it in like every other bastard had. But of course the other bastards weren't as desperate as my mum for a job. Expensive French whore of a husband to keep, she would say, ruffling Gaby's black curls and lighting another fag. Gaby, my dad. We're clattering down the stairs in the hollow orange light. I'll never see my dad again.

I start to cry inside.

* * *

Tube from Seven Sisters, woman opposite me making her face soft when she sees the puppy peeking out from under mum's horrible cardi. It's already September but it's boiling in here, like a sauna, trickles of sweat down my neck, embarrassed in the leather jacket, hope no one I know gets on at Finsbury Park, but it's okay, it's too early for the pubs coming out, too late for crush of clubbers heading into the West End. Just a few sad old bastards, hot and silent, grimacing at the dog as though it's Jesus fucking Christ come down to earth.

Mum spends the entire journey scrabbling around in her bag and muttering to herself, like a bag lady. I look the other way, pretending she's nothing to do with me, and concentrate on staring down the woman going gooey over the dog. She's one of those nice types who probably spend their lives in the fucking British Museum or somewhere staring at dinosaurs' bones, or whatever they do. Hair in a nice style, neat bob, grey, and one of those cloak things you get in Marks & Spencers, like a sort of cape or a giant scarf. You're supposed to drape them casually over your shoulders, I've seen them in *Bella* and *Chat* and *Woman and Home* and *Woman's Weekly* and *Woman* and *Woman's Realm* and all the other pile of old shit my mum carts back from the launderette, and which I have to read fast before she gets out her scissors and cuts out the pictures for her adult literacy divs, piling them into little heaps – kitchen things, outdoor things, family things, animal things, excuse me while I puke. All cut up and in tidy piles, smiling models with hairbands on, pretending to be coping mums with babies in pastel outfits with Teletubbies knitted into the chests of their jumpers, or gloves with bloody pompoms on. It's all bollocks.

Euston, Warren Street, Oxford Circus. Now it's crowded. I'm staring at the backside of some geezer and his crushed linen wife, jawing on about some show they've been to see, glossy programme on display, just in case the rest of us plebs on the train haven't noticed what a pair of classy bastards we have in our midst – *not the best Sondheim I've seen, but pretty damn close, always has something to say about the human condition, so much more satisfying than the usual Lloyd Webber pap, and so refreshing to see something without Sarah Brightman* . . . I remember her, singing some piece of gooey shit on *Top of the Pops* with a blind Italian gink with a beard. Not that I watch

4

Top of the Pops avidly, or anything, it's telly for six-year-olds, but if it's on and I'm in the room. So we listen to these two jawing on about their bloody musical experience and how uplifting it all was, and down the other end of the carriage someone's shouting into someone's face for money and people are getting tense, but when the train stops at Green Park the shouter gets off, and there's a sigh of relief from everyone and a general relaxing of shoulder-muscles. Meanwhile Mum and I haven't said a word. What's to say?

Train gets to Victoria and we get off, Mum with tube tickets in her teeth, dog in the holdall, clutching me by the sleeve of my jacket, though where she thinks I might go I don't know.

Down a windy street to the bus station, where she goes to stand in a queue and I hang about the magazine racks and pull a leaf of *khat* out of my shoulder bag when she's not watching and have a chew. I've only got a bit left, which is a small, dark worry in the back of my head. I start reading an article about a woman who ended up accidentally marrying her brother who had been adopted when he was a baby but stayed in the same town and his mum and dad who adopted him died and then they'd got engaged and had the whole church bit and everything, white dress, bridesmaids and then after that he decided to look for his real mum and found out who it was only it was too late. The magazine didn't say it, but they'd obviously made with the big flesh stick as Oombe says, and she was saying "I'm not ashamed", and saying they were going to go away somewhere and live together on a desert island where no one would care if they were brother and sister, and they could have babies and all that, only the doctor was saying there was the chance of congenital something or other and they were never going to speak to their mum again for causing them so much pain. There are pictures, of a sad fat woman and a little man with a weedy moustache. They've got the same bulging chins and hair like tap water.

One last bit, and I'm going to run out of *khat*, the only thing that keeps me going. I have this terrible feeling I'll never be back in London again, which means no more *khat*. Wherever we're going, I don't think Ethiopian Airlines lands there. Oombe says it comes wrapped in banana leaves and they sell it on the stalls in the High Road in East Ham, and they have to be pretty damn quick because it's only good when it's fresh, so somewhere in Africa there are these geezers roaring around the desert in their jeeps with piles of *khat* in the back, shoving it onto aeroplanes so it can get to the East End in time to get the Somalis high and happy as they sit in their refugee centres and think about the war. I don't know. She gives it to me, I never pay, she pinches it from her dad, he never seems to notice, too busy jawing and boring her shitless about the homeland. Fortunately I don't speak Somali and he speaks less and less in English. When they first got here, he made an effort with me, asking me lots of questions, but now he's dull and silent, listens to the World Service on his little radio, eyes dead, no talking to little white girl any more.

I select a copy of *Hello!*. There's a picture of Cindy Crawford on the front. Finding Spiritual Fulfilment After Her Break-up With Richard Gere. Good boob job.

Mum's moving away from the ticket window looking pleased with herself. I don't look up from the picture of the Queen coming out of Sandringham Church in a red hat and matching coat by Norman Hartnell.

"Bay fifteen," she says. "I'll get us a couple of baps for the journey. You want to hold the puppy?"

I say nothing. Baps! She can be so embarrassing sometimes.

Finally we get on the bus. On the side it says Newcastle Flyer. I don't say anything. My mum comes from Newcastle, or somewhere near there. Maybe we're going to stay with one of those aunties and uncles she's always going on about. Except I thought they'd all fucked off to Australia and America and places, and Mum was the only poor sap who stayed behind, at least that's what she told me once. Still, ours not to reason why, as she so often says, though I don't really know what it means, other than that she says it when Gaby's gone into a rage about something and she doesn't understand what she's done. Only – Gaby, mustn't think about him. Dad. I miss you already. What are you doing?

We've got seats down the back, which is a bad idea

because every time the bus hits a bump we shoot up in the air. I can't believe it's so full. Who are all these people on the Newcastle Flyer in the middle of the night, murmuring in the dark as we bounce along the motorway out of London into the black blackness? I know why we're here. We're here because I did something bad, and she's angry with Gaby so we've got to go away. But why are the others here?

I stare into the night-time flashing by most of the way, my strange *khat* half-awake sleep, shoulder touching hers, and no words between us. There's a point when the bus stops at some service station and she touches me and asks me if I want to go to the toilet. I can't believe she's actually saying the word *toilet* out loud on a bus. I say no. She says she's fed up with being the one who always takes the puppy for a wee. *Wee . . . !* I tell her I don't want a fucking puppy. She starts crying, a slow trickle. The woman sitting in the seat in front who stinks of some floral perfume – I mean really stinks, sickly stench of flowers right up inside your nostrils until you can hardly breathe – she turns round and stares at me with large watery eyes. I grab the puppy, stalk up the bus and get off. It's the middle of the night. We're at one of those giant car parks and eating-places. The driver says fifteen minutes and disappears, yawning, into the dark. I follow a ragged procession of bus passengers into the orange-yellow glare of the service-station foyer, where, giddy, I read the signs: Harvester Restaurant, Bon Appetit

Cappuccino and Croissant bar, Ladies, Games Room, Gentlemen, Nappy Changing Facility, 24 Hour SupaShop, BurgerKing. I put the puppy down on the floor and it skates happily away on its big paws, excited to be free, disappearing round a corner. Goodbye, little dog. I choose the nearest entrance and go in through the automatic doors so it can't follow me.

The shop is still open, with one sleepy boy in a Supashop nylon jacket picking his spots at the counter, one till switched on, with Next Customer Please lit up, all the others wearing funny little hoods over them, like a row of monks' heads on the counter. He glances at me as I wander in. I'm studying these little stretchy tops, white with roses, on a stand at the back, and I'd really like one, but there's no chance of stashing one, he's watching me. I wander away, then head back again, but it's no good, I can feel his eyes on me. He's looking at my body. I turn to stare at him, and his neck suddenly goes red.

"They're nice, they are," he says. He's got some kind of weird accent. "Look nice on you."

"Give us one," I say. "I'm skint."

He laughs, an unnatural, high sound. Self-conscious. Bet he's never done it. "I'd get the sack," he says.

"No one here to see."

He knows I'm right. "So I should just give it you," he says. "Just like that."

I know what he means. "We could do a deal," I say.

9

*Only we'll have to be quick or the bus'll go and then I'll be
really nowhere*.

He's terrified. He can't believe what I've just whispered
to him at the counter. I'm holding the top, size ten. But
he's got to take the security tag off.

He asks me where. He can hardly speak, the word is
stuck somewhere in his throat and the red on his neck
is moving upwards. Acne and blushing. An ugly little
Northern bastard.

He's locking the till with a shaking hand then we go
over to a door at the side of the shop, by the shelves of
Twenty Bestsellers, half the boxes empty. I wonder
fleetingly what book it was at Number Eight that sold so
well in this hole in the universe. Fifty ways to wank,
maybe. He's unlocking the door, and we go in. It's a store
cupboard, peculiarly warm and piled with boxes. Outside,
through a window high up in the wall, I can hear the
deep hooting of a horn. I wonder if it's our bus. Mr
Spotty's standing with his mouth slack, his hands pressed
against the sad blue nylon of his SUPASHOP jacket. He
can't believe this. I can see his lump bulging in his
trousers. I feel strong and full of hatred. I pull off my bike
jacket and he goes to touch me but I say that wasn't part
of the deal, was it. He takes a step back, eager not to
offend at this crucial stage. I pull my shirt off over my
head. The boy is sweating in the heat of the cupboard,
boxes towering above him giddily.

"Go on, then," he says. "Show us them."

"I am."

"I mean – you know. All of them."

I haven't got time for this. "That wasn't the deal."

"You want that top or not?"

Quickly I pull the straps down and yank my bra off. "Here," I say, suddenly ready to explode, furious. "Touch. Go on. Touch!" His hot hand touches. Fingers my nip. I don't care. I watch it expand under his hand. I feel a flicker somewhere in my gut and turn it instead to nothing. I hear a little gasp from him, feel a rough sliver of skin on his thumb as he gets into the swing of things, thumb and finger rubbing me, hurting a bit. I'm going to have to stop or it'll get complicated – him wanting more, me being tempted because I could do with a bit of cash actually, then we'll have to negotiate and then do it, and I haven't got time. The bus.

"That's it," I say briskly. I drag my bra back into position over my nips. It's a good one. Marks and Sparks. Underlift and half-wired, purple. There were matching knickers but they were on a different bit of the stand and I couldn't get them off the poxy hanger and into my bag in time. Deal done, and true to his word, I'll say that for him, he hands me the white top with the roses and I pull it on.

"Yeah," he says, softly, hand out to touch. I swerve away and pull on the leather jacket, then push out of the cupboard and swing the door back hard so it nuts him as he follows me out. He yells in pain and calls after me but

11

I keep walking, across the shiny floor, pleased with myself, catching sight of me in the reflecting window of the Games Room, slinky little top fits well. Good deal.

Back on the bus, the engine running, everyone's on, she's standing at the back, anxious and angry.

"Where's the puppy?"

I'm about to tell her it ran off, a long sad tale I concocted across the car park about me searching BurgerKing and someone saying they'd seen a dead puppy under the wheels of a lorry, only Stench-of-Poppy suddenly climbs in by the driver, all important and puffing, and she's got the puppy squirming under her arm. The bus moves off and the Flower Fairy staggers down the aisle, falling into the corned beef sandwiches open in silver foil on the lap of the bloke two seats further down, sorries and giggles and gasps of joy over the puppy and isn't-he-sweet-whatsis-name coming at us from all over the place. I grab the window seat while Mum gabbles on about no name yet, still trying to see what personality it's got before a name or some such bullshit. She gets on to star signs with the perfumed one, and we're off again along the dark streak of motorway, a cocoon of travellers swaying and rocking in the bouncing bus, past a sign that says The North, as the sky is streaked with gold and the man with the corned beef sandwiches sighs melodramatically and says "Dawn . . . !" And suddenly they're jawing on together, the smelly perfume woman, the man with the sandwiches and the thin stripe of hair placed carefully over his bald

bit, and Mum, sad bundle of red hair with a squashed bit
at the back where she's been sleeping on it, nervous
bright eyes and tinny little laugh. Three intellectuals who
have found each other on the night bus to Newcastle,
poncing on about William Blake and jocund day standing
misty on the mountain tops while the man feeds his
sandwich to the puppy and I make my jacket into a
pillow and stare at my own sad pointy face in the window
of the bus, admiring the curve of my new roses and white
mesh neckline, my brain racing. I'm not going to ask her
where we are going. I'm too scared to hear the answer.
Wherever it is, it's my fault we're going there.

I close my eyes and sink back to the place my head was
before all this started, hours ago, at the end of a good club
night, on the way home in the dark, breathless body and
headspin. Clank up the stairs, buckle on my boot loose,
see a dark cat skulking by the lift doors, know it's not cat
but *khat*. Often see a dark cat skulking – in my brain, out
of the corner of my eye – or is it real? One hope only –
keep the Angel Gabriel asleep. Or that Mum will be
home, but I know she won't be, she's always working.
Islington Adult Education. Reading skills for adults. Or is
it Payclean tonight – two hours at the launderette? I can't
remember. Why should I remember the whereabouts of
my mother when it's Allstars Africa Night? Too much
that *khat* dancing in my skin, making my mouth dry and
jiggling my belly. Key still down my bra. Fish it out, hands
icy, shiver right through me like when you see a lorry

waiting at the traffic lights, juddering, waiting to shoot forward out into the junction, juddering and waiting, that's me.

Key in lock, not too much guesswork, done this a million times. Head full of Somali songs, mad music, grinning teeth and white eyes, black black faces, sweat pouring from their nappy heads, long skinny bodies, arms that go on for ever, dancing like no white boy ever did. Key turn, door open, *attends*!

Sound of the television. ITN, Trevor McDonald, apology of a black man with his posh voice and his shirt and tie. So Mum isn't home – she never watches ITN, says it's for plebs, prefers *Newsnight*. In-depth. More in-depth. Hots for Paxman more like, says the Angel Gabriel. She never answers when he says that. The Angel Gabriel. Gaby. My dad. I try and shut the door with no sound, but I can't. Too much that *khat*. Door clinks, deathly sound, and Gaby calls.

"That you?"

I don't answer.

"Joanna?"

I am standing in the hall. He's waiting for me. I see him in my head, hand on the remote control, sound down – there it goes, Trevor McDonald cut down like a knife.

"Come here. I got a present."

Pretends to be watching tv, sound back up, but I know. He's waiting. He's been waiting all afternoon, watching for mum to go, sharp black little rat turd eyes watching, excited but not showing it, cold. Mum in the hall where I am now, shoving a tortoiseshell comb into her sad, pale red hair, another comb in her teeth, head bowed. Going out now, Gaby. *Uh-huh.* Tell Joanna I expect her to be in bed when I get in. *Oui.* And if she's been chewing that stuff again, tell her I'll know. *Tu n'en sais rien.*

Sorry . . . ? But he'll say nothing, and she'll leave, off to her illiterates in the community centre, deaf to the clues, blind, deaf, dumb. Only me here to cope. It's okay. I'm fourteen. I can hack it.

"Joanna."

I go and stand in the doorway, hugging my jacket round me, arms folded.

"I've got a present for you."

"I don't want nothing." I hear my voice crack, like a stranger's. He's stretched out on the sofa, thick smell of cigarettes round him, a yellowish pall smoking around his head, and on the carpet wine and glass, bottles, ashtray, dope, big brown kitchen-box of matches.

"Come here."

I don't move. My body is electric. I make my face ugly, pinch my mouth, knowing it's no good, knowing it's coming, whatever I do, I can't make this not happen, I've tried everything before, nothing works, the only thing is to get it over with.

"Look – for you –"

I don't look. I know what he wants to show me.

15

"Joanna – here –"

I take a slow step into the room. That's it, over the boundary of the green hall carpet onto the sickening oatmeal swirl of the living-room. Funny thing is, the rest of my life I never notice the carpet, never look at the floor – only at these times, the times of me and Gaby when Mum's out and me and him and me and him and me and him too much that *khat*, churning in my mouth like vomit. I swallow it.

Gaby is grinning at me, showing that funny yellow fang he has, I see it even when his mouth is shut, glinting through his lips, pressing into the flesh of his mouth. He beckons. I go. He wants my eyes to be looking down, I know where, but I look lower, at my own feet, boot buckle dangling, feet of me, looking like feet of someone else. Grown-up feet in grown-up boots, feet of woman. Because I *am* a woman. Now.

"Look."

I look.

It's a puppy. I can't help it, I raise my eyes and they meet his, Gaby's, a crinkle at the corners, smiling his smile.

"A present," he says. It's curled in his crotch, asleep, but raises its head and looks at me sleepily, soft long ears and a pale muzzle, gentle big paws, blond tufts sprouting between pink pads.

"Well, don't just stand there!" Gaby says. "Aren't you going to say thank you?"

This is the whole point, you see. This is where I get to pay for the puppy.

"I brought you a present, and you don't even thank me?" The puppy's stump of a tail is wagging at me, stirring in Gaby's groin. It stumbles to its feet, wobbling. I can see the mound beneath.

"Thank you."

"You don't sound very grateful."

There is no answer from me. What answer could there possibly be to stop this happening? There is none. *Rien.*

"Don't I get a hug?"

The woman's feet in the boots with the dangling strap step softly, so softly on the swirling oatmeal, over to the settee for the hug.

"And a kiss . . . ?"

The kiss.

"Just a minute – I put the dog out, just for a minute –"

He always sounds much more French when it's time. Maybe he remembers someone in France, some girl he fucked once.

"Sit."

He's talking to me, not the dog. Which he has by the loose flesh on its golden neck, feet dangling, helpless. It hangs, limp and trusting, waiting to see what will happen to it next. I wonder what it's like to be that puppy, with your life a blank, mother-dog gone, strange new world, waiting to see what happens next.

I know what happens next. He's put the dog in the

hall. He comes back to his place on the sofa, and as he passes, his hand, hot, on the back of my neck.

"Come and sit with me."

Now I can feel the blood slowing to sludge in my veins, my heartbeat down to a steady, dead throb. Now I can sit and feel his hand on me and hear the murmur of his voice telling me he loves me, I'm his best girl, *chouette*,

He loves me best of everyone, best girl, *de tout le monde*.

* * *

It's Newcastle in the bright morning. We're walking from somewhere called Gallowgate to somewhere called Haymarket through the dusty waking-up city streets, still not speaking, dog is dragging behind on a string the corned-beef man gave us, half-throttled as the string tightens round its fat little neck. We get to another bus station, this one full of different coloured buses, *Arriva* on the side. There's an argument about tides at the ticket window. I don't understand. Are we getting a boat?

"We want the five oh five," she says briskly, walking away from the window. "We've got over an hour."

We eat cheese rolls and KitKats in a sad little canteen with a girl in a brown stripy apron and a white stiff hat behind the counter. She doesn't smile at all. I wonder if she ever does. She doesn't look at us either. If we were murdered round the corner in a dark shadow away from the sun, she wouldn't be a reliable witness. She spots the dog.

"No dogs," she says. Only she says 'naw dogs'. Mum looks flustered. "It's only a puppy," she says. My spine stiffens. She's doing her posh voice, the one she uses for teachers at parents' evening when they're going on about me drinking at the last chance saloon: 'She's only a girl.' That's what you think. The teachers – most of them – know different. You can't be in year twelve and still be a girl at MLK. You have to have a face like a rock, nothing gets past you and no one hurts. Otherwise you go under. Like sad little dweebie Lorna McKenzie, her small black face crumpling because she was alone. And no one to help her, no one to step in and say 'No! leave her alone!'. Days and days of it. Until finally they took her away. We were glad.

"Naw dogs," says the girl again, her voice flat, like she's said this a million times already this morning.

I take the dog and tie it to a creaking Walls Ice Cream sign squeaking outside the door. We sit inside and eat our rolls, both of us staring at the puppy as it strains and cries to get at us through the glass. We're not making small talk. We just eat. "Yeller," she says suddenly. "Like in the film. *Old Yeller*." I look at her. Our eyes meet for the first time since it happened. "Walt Disney," she says, as if that explains everything. "Dorothy McGuire. And Tommy Kirk playing the boy. The boy that loved the dog." Our eyes slide away.

She falls asleep, her chin low on her chest, her mouth slightly open. I've always loved her mouth, so wide across her face, like Louise, her who was in Eternal. While she sleeps I eat the last of her KitKat.

The next bus is going to take us to somewhere called Road End. I hear her talking to the bus driver. Another two hours, only this time it's day and I stare out at sheep, their strange square bodies flashing by in crazy repetitive patterns as I try to focus before we pass, my eyes sliding over the blurred fences and fuzz of hedgerows. Too much that *khat*. We have been bouncing along the back seats of buses forever. I chew my last leaf quietly as Mum fusses over the puppy. She's calling it Yeller. It lies in her lap, ecstatically exposing its soft pink stomach to be rubbed. I think about sticking a sharp pencil into that pinkness. The bus stops a lot, and people get on and off, talking about the weather, wiping the sweaty wetness from their foreheads, damp patches under their arms, flapping and exclaiming over the heat in accents I can hardly fathom. Northern peasants. My white and rosy top is rumpled and grey-looking in the light of day, it's lost the sheen of newness and now I see it's just another cheap bit of tat, like all the other things I've got. Had. They're all at home. Dad. Gaby. What are you doing now?

Suddenly there's the sea, grey and out there, white foam flecking the waves and in spite of myself I'm a little excited. And there's a coolness through the bus, like we've all smelt it at once and the sun has receded while we breathe the salty air. And then we get off. The bus rumbles away and disappears round a bend. I can still hear it as it strains to get up a hill somewhere beyond the hedge. Looking up and out to sea, I'm shocked to see a fairy castle rising out of the mist, waves rolling around it, the sky pale pink, like Disneyland. I can feel my heart beating. It's the most truly beautiful thing I've ever seen. I walk over the road and look across at the castle.

"We want the four seven seven," says Mum inexplicably, sitting on top of her bag, suddenly old. "Here, Yeller, come see Mum," she says, voice lacking conviction, as my drama teacher used to say. Used to say. I liked drama, back at old MLK. Old. My old school. Didn't like much else. The dog is at the end of its string, sniffing at my ankles. I walk out of range.

"The ten forty," says Mum, conversational. "From Berwick . . . " She twigs I'm looking at the castle. "Holy Island," she says. "That's where we're going." I don't answer. Are we going to live in the magic castle?

I wander away round a bend in the road, so I can smoke. I have all the equipment: I got a cigarette I nicked out of her packet on the bus, I got matches and Rizlas in my pocket, I got a bit of dope I stole from my dad yesterday. I'm well equipped.

"Don't go too far, Jo . . . " I just can't look at her. She knows I let Dad put his hand up there, touch me there. She knows. His hand. I feel dirty suddenly. I mean really dirty, like when you scrub and scrub and it's all embedded

21

in your fingernails and won't come out, not unless you poke it with something, scrape it off, hurt yourself in the process.

I'm not here. I'm back in the living-room, on the sofa, with him. Above us, on the ceiling, I look down at Joanna and Gaby, my heart cold. She's doing what he asks and he's gasping a little, she with eyes clenched shut, jaw like a rock. Remember it won't last forever, that's the only comfort she can offer herself, that limp body down there on the sofa, flattened by the dead weight of him, suffocating.

I can hear his mumbling in my ear, "That's it, just a bit . . . For Gaby, mmmn, *extra* . . . " and outside the door the yelp of the puppy, scrabbling to come in, desperate to be back where the warmth is, that's all it knows, the warmth of Gaby, that's what survives in its little dog memory, the last bit of warmth – and me? I am a nothing, a little dot in a great world, shrinking away to nothing so that he won't touch me too much – then suddenly the swish of the door opening, puppy in, light from the hall angled on my upturned face. I open my eyes. Gaby is struggling to get up.

"Jesus Christ." It's my mum. "Jesus aitch fucking Christ."

Gaby is sitting up, shamed hand covering his open trousers, other hand pulling down my shirt. He didn't come. No wetness sliding down my thigh, no cum, no weeping and shuddering into the bones of my shoulder, only the bright light and my mum's expression, her mouth a surprised 'o' in that pale face, red hair angora fuzzy against the hall light. The puppy leaps blindly up and misses its foothold, crashing back onto the carpet.

"You're early," says Gaby, voice shaky. "We were just going to watch *Seinfeld* –"

Mum has somehow got round the sofa, I don't see how, and there's a yelp as she stands on the dog, then she's got me by the shoulder of my shirt and she's dragging me off the sofa, only she's got my hair caught in her hand and I'm in agony, like my scalp is being torn away from my head, and I'm screaming and yelling for her to stop and saying that I'm sorry, but she drags me across the carpet, puppy yelping at her heels, Gaby shouting and standing up, I see him fumbling at the zip on his jeans – stuffing it all back inside – and she's hauled me out into the hall and is manhandling me down the passage. Just at the point where I think I can get to my feet she knocks me down and I lie, winded, by the cupboard under the stairs. I'm so shocked I've gone into my freeze-zone again, the one where I go when Gaby and I do that thing, where Gaby and I – my head is buzzing. Too much that *khat*, I haven't slept, not properly slept, for so long, and now suddenly I'm tired, my bones are jelly, and I can hear someone sobbing quietly and I realise it's me. My mum has never hit me before.

It's a few seconds before I realise she's gone, and I can move my hands from my face. She's back in the living-room and the door slams behind her. I lie in the soothing half-dark, listening to Gaby and Mum shouting, the sound of my lungs, heaving, the stinging in my head. I put a hand down there. It's raw, red and sore, but at least he didn't come, I won't have a baby. I don't know what I think about what's happening in the living-room. I can hear it, every word. I lie on the green cord carpet – small ridges with dust-filled valleys stretching out, details of fluff and crumbs next to my eyes, levelling out to a smooth desert as it flows towards the front door, jumble of shoes by the welcome mat.

The puppy is in there, I can hear its excited yelping under the voices, Mum screaming, Gaby shouting, then pleading, voice softening, lowered, he'll be rubbing her back now, massaging her shoulders, smiling that soft smile we both love so much.

"Suckers for him, aren't we, Jo," Mum always says when he does that. "One Gallic grin and we're putty."

It's nice in the half-dark. Peaceful. Ridges of carpet against my cheek, breathing calmer now. I'm not really listening, but suddenly I hear his voice, rasping in the way it does when he's watching the rugby and someone in the French team's done something really stupid and he can't quite believe it.

"*Putain!* If you think that then you don't know me at all!"

And Mum, voice higher than usual, almost a squeak: "I don't think I do. I don't think I *do* know you –"

And then some bit of furniture gets knocked over and there's the hard, sharp sound of a slap. I wonder who hit who. Then nothing, only the sound of Trevor Macdonald wishing everyone a very good night, and the steady yap of the puppy, hypnotised by the sound of its own bark, yap, yap, on and on.

Then the door opens, feet down the passage. I lie there, wondering what happens to me now. Feet stop. I look. They're Mum's, tights, with a hole in, no shoes, long toes, glimpse of purple toenail.

"Get up," she says. She seems very tall, face small and a long way off. Alice in Wonderland. Eat Me. Slowly I begin to sit up. I feel bruised in the stomach, weary, bones like lead. "Put some things in a bag."

I gape up at her. She suddenly explodes again, hauling me to my feet. "A bag. In your room."

"Where we going?"

She shoves me against the wall and stumbles away towards the kitchen. "What the fuck does it matter?" she shrieks. Gaby has appeared in the doorway of the living-room. He's got the dog by the scruff of the neck again and it squirms, anxious, bright, scared gleam in its eye.

"Take your fucking present," he says to me, and he throws the puppy at me, missing me so it lands with a loud scream after hitting the wall.

I go into my room and slam the door, shutting out the shouts and the dog and Mum and Gaby and the helter-skelter of events, and I lie on my bed with its stupid Ninja

Turtles quilt cover from when I was fucking *nine* (and she wonders why I don't bring friends home!) and I stare up at the poster of the great Fela Kuti with his wives, all bright beads and cornrows and white teeth and red lips and glossy black skin and the most beautiful necklaces you ever saw in your life, and still I don't cry.

Mum storms in, clutching a black bin-liner, opens my cupboard and stuffs things in, breathing heavily. There's a red patch appeared under her eye. Gaby is standing in the doorway. He doesn't look at me.

"This is stupid," he says.

She's got her head stuck inside my wardrobe, scrabbling about. "Stupid, yes," her voice is tight, still squeaky. "You said it. Stupid, that's me. Only now I'm not so stupid, because now you can get on with your stupid fucking media arts lab and your stupid readings and your stupid living poetry and sticking your stupid dick wherever you please only now you won't do it on my money –" She's hurling trainers out of the bottom of the wardrobe, her voice suddenly thick with snot when she says money, a string of mucus trailing from her nose. "Joanna – I said *pack*!"

I find my voice suddenly. "I don't want to –"

She takes no notice. She's sticking a pair of plastic trousers in the bag. "It's no good putting them in," I hear my voice say, sulky. "I don't wear them –"

She hurls them onto the floor. "You won't do it. I'll do it." Her voice is shaking. She suddenly turns and throws my old leather jacket at me, the biker's jacket I got in Camden Market when I was twelve, for God's sake.

"I don't wear –"

She hauls me off the bed, screaming into my face that she doesn't give a fuck what I wear. I'm to put the fucking thing on or she'll beat the living daylights out of me – and she's forced me into it, my shirt all rucking up at the back, the lining cold against my skin. We're going, I'd better grab anything I care about because we're not coming back here ever. Not ever. Ever. Ever.

The spliff is making me feel giddy and I go and sit under the hedge, stick my head between my knees. I feel so tired and yet I don't want to sleep. I feel the vomit rising up and I lean over and puke up in the nettles, trying to keep quiet so Mum won't hear. In between gut wrenches, I hear the puppy yelping in the road.

"It wants you . . . " Mum calls. I don't answer, just grind the joint out under my boot and rest my head on my knees.

Headspin. Not a good idea.

I must have faded away a little, because suddenly she's shouting and I have to get up because the bus is coming, I can hear it. I pick up the squashed end of spliff and stick it in my pocket.

The bus driver is one of those perky old bastards, wants to talk. Calls me hinny. "On holiday?" he asks. I don't answer. Tramp to the back of the bus, embarrassed by Mum who stands talking, while people on the bus twitch and watch, murmuring in those sing-song voices I've heard ever since Newcastle. She's blabbering on about holidays and relatives and this being her spiritual home. I could die. He fusses over the puppy. Mum settles into a seat behind the driver and we move off.

We're halfway across this flat, wet road, mud either side, the castle coming closer. People are walking, big boots and rucksacks, burnt faces, binoculars. We pass someone pointing at the castle, face frozen in a look of joy. I look too. A castle on an island. I thought it was only in my storybooks, the ones I set fire to when Gaby – no, don't think about that. I miss those books. There was one called *Gobelino the Witch's Cat*. I'd always wanted a cat. I'd call it Gobelino. Lino for short. Lino would always be curled up on my bed and when I came in Lino would look up at me with golden eyes and make a little noise, stretch and go back to sleep. Because Lino would love me but in a distant way, not needing me too much, just there all the time. And he gets me a fucking dog.

The bus has stopped, in the middle of nowhere, wind and shining mud all around. The driver is coming down the bus towards me.

"Put that out," he says. He's looking at me, very blue eyes in a weatherbeaten face, grey stubble on his chin. He says *oot*. Put that oot. He means the dog-end of spliff I lit up when the bus got going.

"No."

I look away. I can hear Mum saying my name, people murmuring.

"Put that out or get off my bus." *Ma boos*. I can't explain it, but suddenly I feel tears pricking my eyes. All the time, being told off, it gets you down.

"Did you hear me?"

"I'm not deaf."

"Jo – come on –"

Mum is about to lean across and grab the fag, so I push her away, shouting "Fuck off!", aware there's a gasp from the passengers and a muttering and a horrible embarrassment, which I share. I get up. Pull the window open and throw the dog-end out.

"Satisfied?"

The driver turns away without a word and makes his way back up the bus. No one looks at me. I hear someone say something about Londoners and someone else laughs. Mum heads back to her seat, her back all stiff. The bus starts up and we're off again. Across the shiny black causeway, heading for the magic castle.

* * *

I hate hate hate hate it here, Nanny stupid fucking headcase, Mummy whining drooping, dog yapyapping until I could scream. That's why we're here. Nothing to do with the castle. Just a grim little wonky street called Marygate and a terraced house in a row and Mum hugging a small wrinkled old woman and calling her mam, and telling me this is my nan and this old bag staring at me, not a smile to be seen and saying "You better come away in"; and then I ask to go to bed and I twitch about in a room up high in the house where I have to bend my head when I stand up, and there's a window and I can see a bit of the castle and a field with a wall round it and everyone goes to bed after some talking and I think fine, now I can go, because if this is where I have to spend the rest of my life in this squashed weird house with the empty space outside and the sea all around then I really will die, and I get up and put my jacket on over my bra and knickers and creep downstairs in the dark and hear Nanny and Mum still talking somewhere, voices low and depressed and I open the door and go out and follow the smell of the sea to where the bus came over from the mainland, only the road's gone, there's only sea now – the sea has covered the road and I'm stuck on this island so I leave my jacket on the sand and I step out into the icy water and then I start to wade off towards the dark shape of the mainland ahead and the waves are bigger than I thought but I'm a good swimmer, bronze medal, so I start swimming and the waves are over my head and it's hard to breathe and it's so fucking cold I can't feel my legs but I think I can't turn back I've got to keep going only suddenly there's lights and shouting and a bloody great THING looms up and there are faces looking down at me and then a hook and people shouting and the sea is roaring round my ears and they haul me upwards and I'm dropped onto the slimy deck of a boat and there are these men staring at me like they've captured a fucking mermaid.

"Silly little foocker . . . "

And they brought me back to Nan's and they shouted at me and Mum dragged me upstairs and held me by my hair while she ran a hot bath and the steam filled the bathroom and dripped down the walls and I couldn't even scream no more because my voice had gone and then she hauls me over the side and pushes me into the hot water and scrubs at me till I'm raw and sobbing a throaty sob and Nan comes in and says here it's winceyette and pulls my arms up over my head and then I'm in this warm soft stuff and they put me in a bed with a hot stone thing under the covers that burns my feet and Mum is crying and saying she's at the end of her tether and the light goes out and here I am in the dark.

I haven't slept since yesterday morning. Yesterday. School. Africa All Stars. Tottenham. *Khat* finally drained away from my brain and I know I'm going to sleep forever in this dark, this silent dark, just the rushing of the wind and a black black hole I slide into. I'll run away again tomorrow.

Chapter Two

Troublemaker, troublemaker,
Fetch a pan and a cake we'll make of her.

NORTHUMBRIAN CHILDREN'S PLAYGROUND SONG.

They came here and turned my life upside down. I can't believe your children are still allowed to come and make demands on you when you're nearly seventy. When in the name of God do you get to be irresponsible in your life? I was just getting the hang of it . . .

It was a Tuesday. I was in the front garden, applying a good strong dose of Tumblebug to the lupins, and quietly cursing the wind that had felled two giant sunflowers nearby, laying the bright yellow globes low among the marigolds. My own fault – Billy always says I'm mad to be planting sunflower seeds in that wind, but I can't resist. Every year, from just a packet of seeds I grow my ten-foot

Neanderthals and sometimes I can keep them upright all the way through August. But not this year.

So there I was, down on my knees with my little spray container aiming at the whitefly, and I saw feet on the path by the stricken sunflowers and I looked up and I knew it was one of my children, but I couldn't for the life of me think which one. It's been a while, and at my age to be honest they all start to look the same: I see a bit of me and a bit of Tommy in all of them, and I can tell the boys from the girls, but that's about it. Mind you, it's not that important, really, since I don't see them from one decade to the next. No loss, in my view. Bairns are for rearing and then sending out into the world, like that Chinese saying. Or is it Japanese? Or Red Indian? The trouble with being sixty-eight is the memory loss. It's the most irritating thing. I could punch the wall with it sometimes, never mind the vicar telling me about grace and age coming together. To hell with grace, I tell him. The day I grow old gracefully is the day you can nail the coffin down. Where was I? The saying. Something about children being arrows you fire from your bow. Or was it bullets?

Either way, here was one of them returned to the quiver, hair all over the place not brushed for days by the look of it, and a girl in tow straight out of an approved school, all sulky and chewing and no eye contact. If I had carried on like that my dad would have walloped me so hard I'd not have been able to ride my bike for a week.

"Mam!" Yes, it was definitely one of them. I got up

slowly, pretending it was harder than it was, so I could organise my face into something approaching a welcoming smile, although in my bones I already knew this was a day I could have done without. And I had been expecting Billy. I wondered where he was.

"It's Cath!" she said brightly.

Thank you for that, at any rate. Cathy. The eldest one. I thought she'd gone off to live in France with that slimy French boy she married. She hugged me and I hugged her back, because that's what we mothers are expected to do. I was shocked at the warmth of her embrace. She squeezed, like she meant it. She had thin, bony shoulders. We stepped away from each other and I looked at her face. God, she looked more like Tommy than I remembered any of them looking – same thin nose and freckles, same red hair in a frizz.

"And who's this?" I said.

She pushed the young girl forward, but I still didn't get to see her eyes, only a lot of dark hair hanging over her forehead. She was tall and wearing a lot of daft clothes. There was a small fat puppy on the end of a piece of string as well. Seems to be the fashion these days, dogs on pieces of string. Sometimes they have little neckerchiefs as well, like gypsies.

I was still adjusting my expression, trying to muster enthusiasm; but my mind, irritated by the interruption to its calm pattern, strayed to the baking I was supposed to be starting after my stint in the garden.

"This is Jo. Joanna. Your granddaughter. Jo, this is your nan."

She still wouldn't look at me. "Like a goat," I said dryly. No one had called me 'Nan' in years, not since the second youngest brought his brood over from Australia, and somehow it didn't matter then because they all sounded like a pack of foreigners anyway. They stayed at the Red Lion because all my rooms were full and I couldn't turn anyone away because they'd all booked in advance. It didn't matter, they were only here a few days, then the whole caboodle went off back to Heathrow to get their plane to Sydney or Canberra or wherever it was they went. Last great outpost of the empire, Tommy used to say. Bunch of ex-convicts kowtowing to the monarchy, they want their heads tested. But that was Tommy. Always an opinion.

Silence. "Nice to meet you," I ventured. It was a lie, but you have to make an effort with family, I suppose. Usually I'm not so polite to strangers.

They'd got bags with them, so I knew I was lumbered. Cathy caught me looking at the luggage and started to go on about having this sudden urge to visit, a lot of talk about being a creature of impulse. But I could see straight away there was something wrong. You don't show up and visit your mam after – what is it? – ten years? – fifteen? – without there being something wrong. The girl, Joanna, was looking at me from under her fringe, but the moment she caught my eye she looked away.

"Can you not tread on my border?" I said to her, trying not to sound too sharp. "Only flowers don't like to be stood on. What's your dog's name?"

She looked at me as if I was worse than the dirt in my flower-bed that she'd walked all over the path. Cathy intervened, anxious to steer us both away from a confrontation. She might have forgotten to phone me for the last few years, but she obviously hadn't forgotten my propensity for plain speaking. "He's called Yeller," she said, gathering him up and bundling him into my arms, her face tautened into a smile. "I think he's a Labrador. Isn't he adorable?"

Adorable! Anyone would think she'd just stepped out of some Islington wine bar. Maybe she had. But the idea of me producing a daughter who says words like *adorable* was a little dispiriting. Tommy would turn in his grave. But she always was a mixture of posh and wet, now I come to think of it. The sort of girl who ironed her own school blouses because she said I didn't do it properly. Probably New Labour. The dog was lying on its back in my arms, round belly upwards, paws drooping, for all the world like one of the piglets up at Donald's farm. I'm not a one for pets. I stared at his hopeful face. He tried to lick me.

"You'd better come away in," I said, and headed up the path. I held the door open for them, and as they filed silently past (there *was* something wrong, very wrong) I cast an eye up the way to see if I could spot Billy, but there was no sign. Funny. And I was going to make him some barm cakes to take back, for the journey.

"Kitchen's down the back," I said, putting the wriggling dog down on the hall mat and hoping it wouldn't do a widdle. I followed them down the passage. "I wish I'd known you were coming," I said. "I could have done some baking." *If I knew you were coming I'd have baked a cake*. Tommy used to sing that one when he came back and found me in the kitchen, him smelling of herring and sea salt and me all floury and bad-tempered. Him singing and me pretending to be cross when he put his wet fishy hands on me, and him knowing I wasn't cross at all.

Cathy was looking round, touching things. I tried to quell the flicker of irritation as she picked up a small shell model of the Longstone Lighthouse from above the range and fingered it. I know where everything goes, you see.

"I'll put the kettle on," I said, picking it up and carrying it over to the sink. I turned the tap on hard, so I wouldn't have to speak for a minute, but when I turned back she had been speaking anyway.

" . . . electricity?"

"Pardon?" I put the kettle on the griddle and busied myself with mugs.

"I was just asking if there was any electricity on the island?"

I snorted. "What do you think we are – a bunch of

cave-dwellers? Of course there's electricity, girl. Only I like my old stove. It's better for baking."

I was aware that Joanna, my grandchild, was standing frozen on the flagstones. A stranger in my house. She was plucking at her t-shirt, a skimpy floral thing, picking at a hole in the side seam, her face puckered in concentration.

"That's a pretty top," I said, trying to be friendly. "Wants a bit of mending."

She stuffed her hands in her pockets, pulling her leather jacket close around her and stared out of the back window at my vegetable garden. I had half a mind to give her a basket and get her out there picking the green beans, which is what I'd have been doing if they hadn't showed up, but I decided it was a bit early to be allocating household chores. Anyway, perhaps they'd be gone by the morning.

As I sorted out the mugs and got the biscuit tin and told Cathy where the larder was so she could get the milk, Joanna suddenly spoke.

"Is there somewhere I can crash?" she said. Her voice was surprisingly sweet and little-girl-like. She looked so much like a juvenile delinquent I was expecting I don't know what – a great big booming baritone, I suppose.

"Joanna . . . " Her mother was making a face at her from the larder.

Joanna turned her white face back to me. "Sleep," she said abruptly. "I mean sleep."

"It's all right. You can have the back room. Number three."

I crossed the kitchen and fetched her the key from the row of hooks behind the door. She took it without thanking me, briefly touching my hand with cold fingers, and crashed clumsily out into the passage.

There was a squeak from the dog as she passed it. A well-aimed toe, I thought. I took the milk bottle from Cathy and poured milk into the mugs, listening as Joanna thumped up the stairs. I heard her hesitate on the landing, then the click of the key as she unlocked number three.

I turned to face my daughter. She had sat herself down at the kitchen table and was carefully tracing the whorls of wood with a chewed finger. The door of number three slammed shut upstairs, rattling the horse brasses above the range.

"Sorry," Cathy said wearily. I got the impression that she spent a lot of time saying sorry to people when Joanna was around.

"Did you come on the bus?" I asked. Might as well make a bit of polite conversation while the kettle boiled. She nodded, and I tried not to feel irritated at the realisation that Billy would have seen these two coming in here from the bus stop, and he would have decided to give me a miss. He didn't like hanging about when I had guests. The barm cakes would have to wait.

Cathy sat with rounded shoulders, her finger going round and round on the tabletop, a defeated air about her. If there's one thing I can't abide it's people who let life get on top of them. Eight bairns I had, and a widow at thirty. Where would this one sitting hunched so low at my kitchen table be if I'd let life get on top of *me*? So she's got a delinquent daughter. I had eight. Well – seven. I can't count baby Alice, who died before she was two. Poor wee thing, she never had a chance to be anything much. Just a smiling face and a sick little body.

"So," I said, "have you left that Frenchman? Is that what this is about?"

She didn't look up. "He's not that *Frenchman*. He's my husband."

"Whatever. Is that why you're here? Chuck you out, did he?"

She suddenly looked up at me and I saw a great wash of pain.

"Look –" she said, then whatever it was she was about to say she decided was better left unsaid, and instead she leaned down and pulled a packet of cigarettes out of her shoulder bag. "Do you mind?" she asked, meaning the cigarettes. Normally I do. Guests are allowed to smoke in the living-room only, not in the dining-room and not in their bedrooms. You just get a load of complaints from the non-smokers when they come. Me, I don't mind. The smell reminds me of so many moments. Tommy smoked Players Weights all his life. I got used to the smell. In fact I'd go so far as to say I rather liked it.

"Go on, then," I said. "Seeing as it's you."

The kettle boiled and I tipped a bit in the pot, swilling

it round as I walked to the sink to tip it out. Cathy watched me, blowing a plume of smoke between her lips and suddenly smiling.

"Still strict about warming the pot, then," she said.

"You can't get a decent cup if you don't do it properly," I said.

"No tea bags?" she asked.

I waved the tea caddy at her. It would be the same one she knew as a girl, with the picture of Alnwick Bondgate on the front, only all faded now. "PG Tips," I said. "Never failed me yet."

I could feel her watching me as I made the tea. She was certainly a lot quieter than I remembered, but then perhaps I had just forgotten. It had been so long.

"Fifteen years," she said suddenly, as if she had read my mind. "That's when I last saw you. When I was pregnant."

I remembered then. I was still in the old cottage at Seahouses, and she'd brought that Frenchman to meet me. Said they were getting married. Said he reminded her of James Mason in *The Wicked Lady* – all dark charm and danger. And much too young for her, of course. I was horrified. She was going to have a baby by this young man who didn't even think in the same language as her. Perhaps that's why I had never phoned them when she sent me the card announcing the baby's birth. The card would still be in one of those boxes in the attic. I don't know why I keep all that stuff, I'm not the sentimental type. But you just do, don't you? As if it's your job, keeper of your children's history. Until the day you die and someone else has to do it.

Joanna Marie Thérèse Lefèvre. Can you blame me for not phoning? It didn't sound to me as though this child had anything to do with me and my life. And he was only nineteen at the time, the father. Nineteen. And Cathy was thirty-five. It made me shudder to think about it. The sort of thing that used to get into the *News of the World*. Of course I know it's different now – these people, they're on *Kilroy* and *Esther* and *Oprah* and *Vanessa* and goodness knows what and no one turns a hair, but this was my own flesh and blood. I was glad Tommy was dead the day she showed up with her pretty French boyfriend and her fat pregnant belly. He would never have forgiven her.

I pushed the tea tray across the table and sat down opposite her. This was time I could ill afford. After the baking and Billy's visit, I was supposed to be out putting up the Greenpeace posters in the village hall and outside the church and doing my daily check-up on the guest situation at the Red Lion. It's an arrangement I have with May and Jimmy. The walkers tend to stop at the pub and ask where they can stay; and if the pub's full, then May or Jimmy tells them about my place and gives them directions. Only sometimes the walkers will say "I'll just go up to the Castle and then I'll look in," or if they're religious types – pilgrims, as they like to call themselves –

they might say they're off to the Priory and they'll book in with me later. So I might end up having half a dozen bookings for bed and breakfast that I'm not going to know about until teatime. This way I get a bit of notice and I can do a bit of baking, make sure I've got enough eggs for breakfast, that sort of thing. Good socialists, May and Jimmy.

"She's a handful, by the look of it," I said conversationally, offering Cath a bit of shortbread.

She took a piece and stared at it. Her eyes suddenly filled with tears. My God, I thought, she isn't going to start weeping, is she?

"You still make this," she said in an odd sort of voice, staring at the shortbread and licking the tips of her sugar-covered fingers.

"Of course I still make it. In my sleep. Same recipe my mam gave me when I was a girl."

She bit into it, but her mouth was trembling ominously. "You don't have to tell me anything," I said quickly. God forbid she should break down and start telling me her secrets. "They grow out of it," I said kindly, in an attempt to cheer her up. I worked it out in my head. "Fourteen, isn't she? A nasty age. One half wants to kiss boys, the other half wants to play with her doll's house. You were just the same. And Susan. And the twins."

She looked at me then, mouthful of shortbread, face full of venom. "You mean you remember? You remember what we were like when we were kids?" She stubbed the cigarette out in the ashtray I had supplied her with. "You amaze me. What bit is it you remember exactly? The five minutes in between you coming in from work and nipping out to your union meeting? Or the two minutes when you came in from your job in the pub and shouted at us if we hadn't done the dishes to your satisfaction?"

I stood up quickly. I hate scenes. And my kitchen is my kitchen. It's not something out of *EastEnders*. If she wanted to make a scene she could go elsewhere.

"Look," I said, in a voice as reasonable as I could muster under the circumstances, "you've had a long journey, and I've got things to do. Why don't you go and have a lie down, eh? I'll go and get on with my chores and I'll forget what you just said. All right?"

"Not in the same room. Don't put me in with Joanna."

I didn't comment on this outburst. I handed her the key to number six and stepped out into the passage, narrowly missing the puppy. It wagged its tail at me and fixed me with a look full of hope. I felt a terrible desire to boot it in the backside, and pulled my apron off, furious with myself. They had hardly been in my house ten minutes and I was turning into one of them.

The sun was still high above the sea, and the tourists were watching Johnny and Davy Redpath mending their nets, a thunderous clicking of fancy cameras and oohs and aahs. Johnny caught my eye and winked. Nothing like a ruddy-faced local in thigh-high waders to set the visitors' hearts racing.

The Red Lion was quiet, just May at the bar serving some Japanese, and Jack from the castle garden in the corner by the fruit machine, drinking his customary bottle of Budweiser and minding his own business. He's a Yank, but I don't hold that against him. He's a whizz on wildflowers – hasn't been wrong yet. Find me a man who can tell his Water Poppy from his Hop O' My Thumb and I'll know he means business in the garden. The only area where we fall out is the organic question. When he's feeling mellow he'll have a go at me about chemicals, and how can I be in Greenpeace and still have a shed full of Malathion Dust. But most of the time he stares into nowhere and says nothing and everyone leaves him alone. Speak when you're spoken to, that's the byword on the island, and Jack doesn't often speak.

May looked up and saw me in the doorway.

"Quiet today," she said, which meant no candidates for the B & B.

"Bus gone?" I asked.

"Billy came by," she said. She knows something's going on with me and Billy, but we've never discussed it.

"Right," I said, and left.

I pinned up my poster outside the church, careful not to invade the territory occupied by this week's homily from the Good Book. Bright orange. Big fat letters, like you see when a shop has a sale on. Perfect Love Casteth Out Fear. Only the vicar and I have been known to have words, since he thinks I'm a wicked commie, which I am, and communism is a close relative of devil-worship in his view. So I'm allowed to put my lefty posters on his notice-board as long as I don't go all militant and try to obliterate the word of the Lord. This one was about whales. Not that you get many Great Whites popping into the island for a visit, but you can always get the islanders interested in creatures from the sea. Perhaps there's a feeling that we're all related. The picture looked good next to the orange Bible poster. Ironic. They're still whaling in Norway, aren't they? So much for perfect love.

On my way to the village hall I had to pass right along Crossgate, and people said hello, as they always did, but I felt them looking at me out of the corner of their eyes as I passed, wondering what I'd done with my visitors. It's a small place. Within a minute of those two getting off the bus the Redpath lad would have watched them go into my house, would have maybe seen me taking them inside. He would have told his dad, who always has a pint at the Red Lion at lunch-time if the fleet isn't out, so everyone would have known before May had pulled the handle on the pump. Not that I minded people knowing. After all, Cath and her brat would probably be off in a couple of days. It was just the disturbance factor, the ripple in the pond. The prodding with a stick at the smooth edges of my life, so hard won. An oasis at the end of a long struggle. And now these two.

I wasted time in the village hall talking to a couple of washers-up left over from the WI, Nancy and Mary. I could tell they were surprised – I'm not usually one for conversation, but I just had a terrible reluctance to go back to my kitchen, where the aliens had landed. I helped them dry the cups and stack them in the cupboard, and we talked about the Verbena Hotels takeover bid, or whatever it's called. No problem there. The whole village is fired up. I could advise them all to form a barricade out of lobster pots and lob grenades at anyone who looks like they might work for a hotel chain, and they'd do it. Even the vicar's gone all Man of the People and said I can count on his support, whatever that means. So much for the march of time. They can march away on the mainland, but they're not bringing their daft ideas across here. Of course I'm really in this for May and Jimmy, because a Verbena Hotel on the island would put them out of business. No, I'm lying. I'm in it because I like a good scrap, and this is going to be a good one.

Finally I had to go home. They were locking up the hall, and my stomach was telling me it was teatime.

Cath was up and about, and had fetched some coal in, which I took to be a hint, so I made us cheese on toast to eat by the fire, even though it was summer. A fire can be a comforting thing I've found, particularly for people from London. The puppy stretched out in front of the hearth, ecstatic and dozy. No sign of the girl. Cath said this was normal – sometimes she slept all weekend. Didn't sound very normal to me, but it was none of my business so I ate my toast and said nothing.

We watched the news on Channel Four as the sun streaked the sky and the seabirds whooped and cried in a last outburst before dark. Cath said she always watched *Brookside*, so we watched that, although I had no idea what was going on, and kept thinking I ought to be baking, but it seemed rude to suddenly get up and fetch the cookery books, so I stayed where I was.

No sound from upstairs. Cath smoked cigarette after cigarette and stared into the flames, and I sat quiet wondering if she would talk to me and hoping she wouldn't. I'd got a new Catherine Cookson off the library van and it was burning a hole on my bedside table upstairs.

Finally, after carrying the plates out to the kitchen (but not washing them up, I noticed), she returned and sat down again in the old armchair, only this time sitting forward, her hands twisting on her knees, her back rigid. Oh dear. Confession time.

"I expect you're wondering –" she began.

I interrupted her. " Always welcome here. You know that."

She gave me a tired look. "I've left him," she said.

There didn't seem to be anything to say to that. I sat there, wishing I'd put the kettle on before she started. I was gasping for a cup of tea. I always have a cup at seven thirty then another one at nine, and that's the last. Otherwise I spend all night creeping about on the landing on trips to the toilet, which is all right by me – I've got the knack after all these years, I can do the business and then be back in bed and asleep before the flush has subsided; but when I've got the guests – it doesn't do to be wandering about when there are strange men in the house.

The silence stretched between us. She was looking at me, but I couldn't look back. It was too painful, too much of Tommy staring across the years at me. Instead I studied her feet. Neat little feet, like mine. Feet inherited from me. I tried to remember them as baby feet, but it was impossible. I just kept seeing baby Alice's feet in the hospital, pink and healthy, while her face shrank away to nothing. Dear little baby Alice, love of my life and we never even got to sing 'Happy Birthday' twice.

Cathy started to talk then, in a low murmur, almost soothing. I found myself struggling to keep my eyes open. She said it was irreconcilable differences. Paths no longer converging. The age gap. Mutual interests disintegrating.

"Did he hit you?" I asked.

She straightened up, irritated. "Of course not! Honestly, Mother, why do you always have to imagine some primitive working-class scenario –"

Mother!

"Maybe it's because I am working-class," I say drily.

She bowed her head, not rising to the bait. "It was just the usual marital difficulties people have. Plus Joanna hitting puberty."

I snorted a little. "Puberty! Is that what they call it

nowadays? I had four girls if you remember – you think I need telling about teenage girls?" I always say four girls, not five. Little Alice never became a girl, stuck forever in a baby's body. Cath was lighting another cigarette. "And as for the usual marital difficulties –"

She put her hand up abruptly to stop me speaking, like a schoolteacher. "I know what you're going to say, about you and Dad and all the crap you had to put up with. I know all that. But it's different now – women don't have to tolerate unhappy marriages."

I could have slapped her stupid little pinched, ignorant face. "Me and Tommy – we were happy," I said. "Twelve happy years."

Cathy grimaced. "Pregnant almost every year, him out with the fleet all the time –"

"Aye, happy! We made do with a lot less than your generation –"

She groaned. "Spare me the golden memories, please! I was there, in case you'd forgotten. He used to smack you around after he came back from the pub –"

That was it. I stood up, faster than I should have done, and felt my left hip click. Once. He hit me once. And it was because we couldn't find the rent money that week. Her with her Islington voice and her half-educated brain and her excuses for a shabby, failed life.

I don't know what would have happened then if there hadn't been a knock at the door. I say a knock – it was hammering, and men's voices shouting. Cathy and I stared at each other, then I hurried away down the hall, the stupid dog clambering after me, and with a rush of summer air the Redpath boy and Jamie Lang, still in their waterproofs and the sea streaming off them, were shouldering their way in, carrying what at first I took to be a corpse. Then I saw it stir and groan and saw it was Joanna.

Only for me it was suddenly nineteen fifty-nine and the lads from the Seahouses fleet were at the door, red-eyed and wet to the bone, telling me that they'd lost my Tommy in rough seas beyond the Pinnacles, off Staple Island. They couldn't look me in the eye, because they had failed him, they hadn't seen him go over the side. I sent them back to unload the fish. Life must go on. A week later, when the storm subsided and the gales had crossed over to Denmark, his body washed up on the Ness End, here on Holy Island. Strange. I was born on Holy Island. I moved to Seahouses when I married Tommy and I always thought I'd die there. Me and Tommy, together in the churchyard. I suppose that's why I moved back here. Tommy may be buried in Seahouses churchyard, but in my mind I always see him on the sand at the Ness End, still wearing his oilskins, red hair black with seawater and seaweed, his blue eyes open staring at the wide sky and the swirling circles of squawking Brent geese. His body came here, where I was born, and that's why I came back.

I've always lived by the sea, but you never get used to

the drownings. She had tried to drown herself, I suppose. Her legs were blue and her entire skinny body shivered and shook while I tore the clothes off her and Cath, weeping all the while, got the bath ready, and the lads stood around embarrassed and fondled the dog and avoided my eyes.

We forced her to drink hot chocolate although she was nearly sick with it, and we scrubbed at her in the hot bath until the blue dots on her flesh turned red, then I gave her one of my best winceyettes and tucked her up with a stone bottle and flicked the light off. I pondered on the wisdom of calling out Doctor Hunter from the mainland, but there would be fuss and a boat would have to go, and there would be to-ing and fro-ing and everyone on the island talking – not that they wouldn't be talking anyway, with Johnny Redpath chief witness and major tattle-tale. I decided to wait until morning. The icy sea would either have killed her or cured her by then.

Cath was downstairs by this time, standing in the hall weeping all over the two lads, who were both beetroot and anxious to be away back to the boats. They told me they thought it was a boggle they had seen bobbing up in the water, and how Johnny's dad had started reciting the Lord's Prayer, until Jamie Lang had realised it wasn't a ghost at all, it was a drowning girl.

They were keen to go, and I didn't discourage them. "I'll have your medals ready for you in the morning," I said, giving them a wink, embarrassed by Cath, who kept saying they'd saved her daughter's life, and she didn't deserve it, and what good people they were, true heroes, real men – and all the while Jamie's acne turning to puce and Johnny grinning from ear to ear. It would be all over the Red Lion five minutes after opening time.

I shut the door. Cath stood, still weeping, her head against the floral wallpaper, suddenly a child herself.

"You should get to bed," I said. "It's been quite a day."

I watched her go slowly up the stairs, the dog wriggling under her arm. There seemed to be no point in keeping her up. She wasn't going to tell me what had been going on. It's the way of our family. We don't talk about the big things.

At last. My own company, a nice cup of tea and a sit by the fire watching the last red coals slip through the grating into the ashes beneath.

I can't have this, I thought. Tomorrow, they'll have to go.

Chapter Three

They fuck you up, your mum and dad . . .

PHILIP LARKIN, *This Be the Verse*

No telly. It's driving me insane. Watching telly in my bedroom, that's what I always did. In at four o'clock, settle right down to *Montel Williams*, *Neighbours*, *Home and Away*, *Roseanne*, *Hollyoaks*, then Mum yelling it's supper and then back up again for *EastEnders* and then straight through to bed, always something to keep an eye on, and then late films and talk shows into the night when the *khat* takes over and I'm dry-eyed and sleepless. It's what we talk about in the back of the cloakrooms and along the corridors all day. It's what we all gossip about, all of this, like it's our life, which it is. Bright colours of *The Big Breakfast*, Johnny and Lisa Tarbuck, fat blubbery American on *Jerry Springer* screaming at her husband who's been screwing her mother, shadowy profile of a paedophile on *Trisha*, audience of parents of children he interfered with wild-eyed and panting for blood, people doing up each others' living-rooms and hating them, spotty oiks on docu-soaps, Alan Titchmarsh, soft porn on Channel Five, woman in a wedding dress gets stuck in the lift with her ex-boyfriend and they end up fucking right there on the floor of the lift with the bridal party waiting in the foyer, only most of the film is these two writhing about in the lift gasping and moaning, total crap, only it turns out half the girls in the class watched it so we're all hysterical when Oombe says the woman who did the writhing looks exactly like Miss Dyer our French teacher, Dryarse the boys call her and we all end up in detention for not being able to stop laughing in French only of course none of us go so then it's a double detention but we won't go to that either. The only telly here is in a room called the visitors' lounge, and the old bag only puts it on for *Channel Four News*. I can't sit in there anyway. All that flowered wallpaper starts moving in on me. I'm being throttled by roses on trellis-work.

All right, so I didn't go. By the time I got up, the tide was in and we were cut off. At home I have my Bart Simpson alarm clock yelling at me to get up and he says get up ten times before it goes to snooze and he says "Hey, man, aren't you out of bed yet?" and I'll crawl out and somehow be ready for school if me and Oombe have decided to go that day. But here there's only the sea and the birds and Nan shuffling in the kitchen – how am I supposed to wake up? I can't believe it. They all get stuck here. Happens all the time, says Nan, matter-of-fact. You get used to it. Get used to watching the water creep across the road, like a little puddle and then a bit stronger, more and more until the road disappears and there's the pale water and then the dark water and then the waves and it's hard to ever believe there was a road there in the first place. Get used to it, she says.

It's been a week now. Nan stares at me all the time, in that disbelieving way she has, like the first night when the fishermen brought me in, staring at me with her bright blue eyes in that wrinkly old face, ripples of wrinkles round those hard, bright eyes. Like I'm a creature from outer space. I can tell she doesn't like me. Whenever I answer one of Mum's naggy little queries I hear old Nanbread muttering away in her dark old kitchen about respect for your elders and betters. Like the two go together – elder means better. In her world, not in mine. And that first morning I heard her yelling downstairs, and that's what got me out of bed, her shouting about her back being broken and me standing at the top of the stairs looking down while she flailed around like a beetle in her floral pinny, legs in the air, light shining through the glass of the front door, Mum trying to drag her upright, something about slipping on the flagstones in the hall where the dog had peed. She had been answering the door to one of those men who brought me back. He found my leather jacket on the beach. There it was, under her arse. I fell about.

And now there's just me and this god-forsaken hole with a fairy castle plonked on top of it, out here, with the windy sea and the great crashing waves and the rest of the world not very easy to get at. I like the castle, though. I bet it's good in the winter, when there's no one about. It would make a brilliant club. I have these dreams, about bringing Oombe here, and we start up our own Africa Allstars and there are fairy lights strung along the battlements and glittering in the windy dark, and the sound of Somali Jazz played very loud drowning out the crashing waves, and all those grinning faces and the sweet smell of sweat and all moving together and everyone shouting *Shubahada*! And the sheep looking up from their eternal choppers-in-the-grass position and being surprised for once in their dull sheep lives.

No music. I never brought my Walkman or any of my CD's. I wish I'd thought at least to get them to Oombe, so someone could have a bit of pleasure from them. She always wanted my Waaberi CD and now it's rotting in my bedroom and no one to have any pleasure from it. I wonder if he's been in my bedroom. I wonder if he's sorry that what we did means he won't see me no more, nor Mum. My mum. She sits at the kitchen table in a kind of sozzled half-world, drinking old Nanbread's Scotch and watching her chopping vegetables with her gnarly old

wet hands. I sat on the stairs last night and listened. I
wanted to know if Cath – Mum – was going to tell Old
Wrinkly about what she saw when she came in from
wherever she had been that night, if she was going to say
about me and Gaby and all that. But all I heard was her
droning on again about being made redundant, twelve
years at the BFI which stands for British Film Institute
and then they restructure the Archive. I can recite it
word for word, I've heard her giving the same speech to
her skinny Jewish friend with the little pink glasses and
to the Adult Education Co-ordinator who comes round –
came round – to sort out their dreary little lessons, a fat
woman with small eyes who smiled at me a bit too much
for my liking. Creeparse. I hate it when old people try
to be friendly. Anyway, it's the same old same old:
preservation and access and corporate sponsorship
dictating culture or somesuch, and the old woman just
grunts occasionally but doesn't say anything much. There
are long silences. I can hear the glug of Mum pouring
herself another whisky and then a sigh. I go back up to
bed.

I hate this island. It's windy all the time, I can never
do a decent hairstyle, I step outside the door and it's gone,
wind whipping my hair across my face in rat's tails.
There's only a few old people here, and a load of sheep,
and then a busload of gawping tourists when the tide's
out and the traffic can get across. I don't go out much at
first, because it's too fucking windy, but the old bag keeps

pushing me out with the dog and telling me to get some fresh air. Fucking little dog.

"He likes you!" Mum keeps saying. "Yeller likes you!" and it's true. Watches me with anxious brown eyes, so two pairs of eyes following me about, her at the kitchen sink washing leeks, stupid puppy sat on the flagstones, its fat pink belly displayed, big feet relaxing on the tiles, gazing gazing at me, while Mum stares into her glass of booze or shuffles about rearranging the photographs on the dresser. They're all her brothers and sisters. "Is this really Jessie?" she'll say, or "Did you say these three were Davy's boys?" They're all over the place – Canada, Melbourne, one in Ireland. I don't remember meeting them, or all these clean-faced brightly coloured children smiling out of the frames, all of them my cousins, all looking like they have proper magazine lives, with proper mums and dads and good school reports and swimming certificates and girl-guide uniforms and tidy toy boxes and clear, clean lives. Nan doesn't seem too sure who is who either – I swear she said one pixieface boy was the child of the one in Melbourne, and then the next time Mum asks, he's suddenly become a Canadian and belongs to an entirely different family. She doesn't seem too interested in them, all these grandchildren and their parents, considering she's got this little gallery of pictures sitting there.

Anyway, as I was saying, she shoves me outside for fresh air and I shove the dog into the little cupboard place round the back where she keeps coal and then I go off by myself. Usually I go up the hill to the castle, and take one of Mum's fags to smoke. There are these three upturned boats that have doors in them and seem to be storerooms, and one of them has a rusty padlock which I work at for a while, smashing away with a big stone until it's open and I can sit in there with the cobwebs and a rusty old mower and some sacks of something smelly and drift away, not thinking about anything really, just knowing that this is what it means to be unhappy, to be lonely and small and have no one, to have your world collapse, which might not have been a fabulous world or one that anyone else would want, but it was yours and you got along all right. I've bitten my nails right down and I study my hands a lot, looking for a spare little flap of flesh to gnaw at. Half the time I don't even know I'm doing it.

When I lie in my poxy little bed with its seven tons of blankets and its peach-coloured eiderdown and its fucking bedspread, I think about my dad, there in the private dark of my own last little private space, and I wonder if he's thinking about me, and then I tidy the question away, because it doesn't have an answer.

One night there's a lot of scraping and shuffling and moving of things above my head, and so I get up and go onto the landing, wondering if there are giant rats sorting out a new existence for themselves up there and it's going to be like in those books where the rats take over and human beings are the scum beneath their feet. Nan is passing at the bottom of the stairs and pauses, looking up at me. The dog seizes the opportunity to race up the stairs and try and get into my bedroom but I shove it back down with my foot and it gives a desperate little yelp of pain. Nan picks it up automatically and strokes it. She's given up lecturing me on how I should love the dog.

"It's only your mam," she says. "Gone up to the attic, sort out a few boxes." She moves away. I hear a loud bump above me and Mum cursing, so I open the funny little low door to the attic and climb up the winding stair. Mum is sitting on the floor, her arms in a big cardboard box with RADIO RENTALS stamped on the side, and all this mess of papers and pictures and files and books all around. Also, of course, the large glass of amber nectar and the bottle of Bell's next to it, half-empty.

"My past spread out before my eyes," she says. Her words are a bit slurry – not enough to make you horrified, just enough to let you know that she's not quite all there. Once the clock in Nan's kitchen tings six o'clock, that's it. She says the same stupid thing in this tense little bright voice about the sun being over the yard-arm and heads for Nan's pantry, where she seems to keep her stock of booze, and Nan never says a word, just looks, and when Mum offers her a drink she just shakes her head and says "Bit early for me". Not for me, though, I always say, hopeful, but Nan glares and Mum sighs and I get zilch, or Nan saying something about whatever's wrong with ginger beer, whatever that is.

She's staring at a photograph and, seeing me looking, she flicks it at me suddenly and I catch it. It's a picture of her, with her beautiful bright hair, smiling, eyes narrowed against the sun, big wide mouth in a grin, and she's on a swing or something, and she's wearing this incredibly short little bright blue dress and flat silver shoes. Silver! And she's got really thin little brown freckly arms clutching onto the ropes of the swing and she's pushed herself away from whoever the person is taking the photo and her thin brown legs are stretched in front of her and she looks so young and bright I can hardly believe it's her.

"Look like you," she says, drinking a glug of booze.

I have another look. I can't see it myself. Never catch me on a swing.

"I was sixteen," she says. Another swig. I continue to look at the picture, not knowing what to say. "Just before I left Northumberland, in fact." She's back rooting in the box and doesn't seem to require an answer. In fact she's obviously forgotten I'm there. I drop the picture into the general muddle of stuff near the box and head off, but she calls me just as I reach the door and she's unrolling some big picture, holding it up.

I stand and look at it. Her hands are shaking a bit and the picture isn't staying still, but I can see it all right. It's someone – at first I think it's a girl, a sixties girl, because of the big heavy floppy blond fringe, but then I decide it's a boy, it's definitely a boy. Big soft mouth. Brown eyes. Straight nose. Serious.

LILIE FERRARI

Looking right at me.

"Scott," she says. "Walker. The love of my life. The real love."

"Great," I say, in my best abrupt and sarky voice and off I go. I clatter down the stairs to blot out the sound of what seems to be my mother erupting into horrible snot-filled sobs of despair, sitting up there like some fucking addled witch with her bits and pieces. On the landing I can hear the telly in the visitors' room. Nan's watching Des O'Connor. This is like suicide. I go to bed.

* * *

I'm eating a bit of toast late next morning and Mum isn't up and Nan's making her by now usual speech about how we don't seem to be able to get up until lunch-time, and then someone's knocking on the front door, just as I'm busy asking her who is Scott Walker, and as she heads for the hall she pauses and looks at me.

"Scott W–?" she says. Then she makes that funny little snorty noise when she thinks something's a load of crap. "Och, *him*. He's the reason she called you Joanna." I stop eating toast and wonder if I heard that right, only I can't ask any more, because there's a bit of excitement when the knock at the door turns out to be this bloke showing up wanting a room. It's a Bed and Breakfast, Nan's place, only no one ever seems to stay there, not surprising since she doesn't advertise anywhere and there are no signs. Best-kept secret on the island she says, like

64

this is a great thing. Anyway this Bannion, this man, he turns up with his bags and I can see Nan doesn't want him there and that they've met before. I'm standing in the kitchen doorway, and I hear everything.

"I'm full," she says.

"That's not what they told me at the Red Lion," he says. He's small, in a suit, with a pleased grin like a boy, although he's pretty old, over fifty at least. He's holding a bag with Adidas written on it, like he's about to go off and play a quick round with Tim Henman or something.

"You wouldn't like it here," Nan says, arms folded. I can't see her face, but she's squaring her shoulders, like Les Dawson on UK Gold when he's being that old woman with no teeth.

"No choice, Mrs Weatherson. Pub's full. I'll just have to lump it." He's pushing his way in, and catches sight of me and flashes that grin in my direction. I move away and go round behind the kitchen door, so he can't see me but I can still hear. "Is that another guest I just spotted? I thought you lived here alone."

"Family," Nan is grunting. She says it as if this is a word she isn't familiar with. "I suppose you'll have to have the front upstairs. It's only a single bed, mind."

"Fine." I hear him take a few more steps in, just to make sure. "I'm not expecting to hit lucky, not in this neck of the woods." He snorts a bit, like this is a joke, but Nan is busy ushering him into the kitchen, her face rigid, her mouth, usually weirdly wide and soft like Mum's, is now a tight line. "Visitors' book is in here," she says. He's looking at me and smiling.

"Hello," he says. I go cold, and walk past him and out into the hall.

"Don't mind her," Nan says. "She's fourteen. Sign here."

I find out his name later, when they're all in the front room watching the news. It's scrawled in long looping fancy strokes, like he's read one of those articles about telling your character from handwriting and he's decided he wants to come in the category of 'thoughtful, artistic, sensitive' only of course it doesn't do anything of the sort. It tells you he's a poser, plus next to 'Occupation' he's written 'Hotel Management, Verbena Group' and I don't remember the likes of Byron having much to do with hotel management. Byron the poet, Lord Byron, 'She Walks in Beauty', we did it at MLK in English and Miss kept going on about how he was the Gary Barlow of his day and we all tried not to smirk, because only teachers would imagine that a load of fourteen-year-old girls would have the slightest interest in some old lag from Take That. But Byron was sensitive, and they say he fucked his sister, which I thought was interesting. Dennis Bannion. You can have the loopiest handwriting in the world, but you can't fool anyone with a name like Dennis.

Anyway, I wouldn't be telling you all this, only an emergency arises when that same evening, after old Bannion has stopped trying to be important with his mobile phone all over the place and has gone up to his room, I'm checking Mum's purse for change, which I'm collecting towards the bus fare to cross the causeway and get the fuck out of here, when Nanbread comes in and catches me counting out the pound coins and all hell breaks loose. It's like I've committed a murder. She carries on like she can't believe I'd do such a thing, stealing is the lowest of the low, and who in God's name taught me to go filching other people's hard-earned money, and then Mum comes in and asks what the fuss is about and then when Nan tells her they start arguing, because Mum is saying she's sure Nan's wrong, I was well brought up and I'm an honest girl, and then it turns into a big screaming session about Gaby and what a useless lummox he is according to Gran, and see what he's produced, a little French thieving thing, nothing like the rest of us, only she says 'oos' instead of us, and then Mum says what would she know about the rest since she was never a mother to any of them, so who is she to start giving lectures on the upbringing of children. It's no good me hanging about, because Mum's holding the purse and the pound coins have gone back in it. I try to slide out of the room, but the old bag grabs me by the shoulder and drags me back in and starts going on about how I'm not human, I treat that damn dog like a piece of dirt and I say I never wanted a fucking dog and then it's a whole new avenue of argument, all about my foul mouth and talking like a whore, only she says 'who-er' and what in God's name happened to childhood and Mum says I don't know you tell me, I sure as hell didn't have one, what with you at your bloody branch meetings playing Joan of Arc to a bunch of fish-factory workers, and Nan is telling her to stop swearing, it's disgusting in front of a child, by which she means me. I can hear Bannion coming quietly down the stairs and I hear his footsteps pause somewhere near the bottom, listening, and while Nan gets into her stride about what really matters in the world and how fighting for the working man is a better way to spend your time than glueing together bits of old film and Mum is saying she's never glued a bit of film in her life and that film culture is more precious than some old job gutting dead fish and Nan is exploding, I manage to get away this time and out into the hall.

Dennis B is standing there, grinning like an idiot and I get that cold feeling I get and say nothing. I'm going upstairs, only he won't move to let me pass so I have to kind of slide round him and I feel his hip moving slightly towards my stomach as I press against the wall and then of course I *know*, and in the moment that I know I also see a new source of income to help me with my bus-fare project, so just for a moment I turn and look back at him and, like I thought, his eyes are on the hem of my skirt just where it meets my bare thighs so I put my hand there and just touch my skin lightly and then I do my Princess Di eyelashes thing, and I hear him breathe a little, a small gasp, and he's in the palm of my hand, I know it.

"Escaping World War Three," he says to me, trying to make his voice sound normal, casual.

"Going to my room," I say. His eyes are on my tits. He looks at me quickly, not sure what he's doing, but I meet his gaze and deliberately look down at myself. Then very slowly I rub my hand over my right tit, so the nip stands up through my cotton t-shirt. I keep my hand there, just under where I know there's a little betraying bulge, and I look at him again. He can hardly believe his eyes. This is always the weird bit for me, because I'm in charge and a little bit of me is excited by this but at the same time I'm a blank, knowing I can do this dirty thing. And people like him run the world. Or at least Verbena Hotel Group.

I go on upstairs, and I know he's standing there, staring after me, wondering what the fuck to do now. And I'm taking a gamble, but shit, I want to get out of here and he's got money, so when he appears in the doorway a few seconds later, pretending to be casual and having some question about where the towels are or some such I don't mess about, because I mustn't think about this or I'll stop and I can't stop because I can't stay here, not with them shouting like that all the time, and the dog always looking at me like it remembers things, so I tell him I'll give him a blow-job for a tenner and he says no a fiver and we settle on eight quid and there's the usual argument about whether I get the money first or do the business, but I know I'm on a winner here so I say it's up to him but I'm doing nothing till I get the dosh, so he gives it to me, trembling fingers in his wallet, one fiver and three coins and I put it on the dressing-table under the sad little flowered doily in front of the mirror, and then I lock the door and he's unzipping his flies and he's sweating and I think he's a sad little bastard, Dennis with a big stick and I'm supposed to suck it and he's sitting on my bed, legs apart on the candlewick which is a bit disgusting but I know I haven't got time to argue about location, so I kneel down in front of him and fondle it a bit, playing for time and he's murmuring and groaning and saying come on come on *come on come on* over and over again and I've just frozen my brain and gone into that blankness and put my lips round the beginning of the great ugly swollen purple Thing and then there's a loud knocking and he leaps up and it's Nan on the other side of the door saying What in God's name is going ON in there and he's cramming it back inside his trousers and I'm standing up and saying I was just showing Mr Bannion the view of the castle from my window and she says let me in at once and Bannion's blathering about how he thought he might like to swap rooms with me but now he's decided he's better off where he is and she's jiggling away at the doorhandle and I run to unlock it and open the door and she's standing there, out of breath and we're all frozen for a second. Then she steps inside.

A very long moment. "Why was the door locked?" her voice goes up at the end, always a question in her voice, even when there isn't one. Only this time there is.

"Handle jammed. Wasn't locked." She won't look away from me and I'm hypnotised, eyes meeting eyes, hers boring into my brain.

Dennis Bannion starts wittering as he sidles out about his room and the view and the joys of island living and Nan tells him he can pack his bags and go now before she calls the police. He hesitates for a second and looks like he's about to say something but then she says "Now!" in this huge booming voice and he goes, leaving me and her doing our staring match, like in *A Fistful of Dollars*, Mum used to get these videos and go on about the Sergioleonetrilogy and let me watch Clinty Eastwood all cold-eyed and staring the other guy down, and suddenly a bit of me wants to giggle.

"You know something?" says Nan, her voice suddenly quiet. I don't answer, because when adults say do you know something they're not wanting an answer, they're just going to tell you something unpleasant you probably don't want to hear. I wait, trying not to let the corners of my mouth move upwards. "I feel sorry for you," she says. "Really sorry. And for God's sake tidy this room." Then she goes. I can't believe it. I thought I was about to get my head chopped off at the very least. The door closes. I hear her footsteps going downstairs. I lock the door again and sit at the dressing-table. I'm going to do the front bits in cornrows on my forehead, and crisscross them with some green string I found in the upturned boat shed. I start humming. I'm eight pounds richer. I can go.

* * *

So now I'm dawdling down what passes as the main street in this place, to the other end of Marygate where I've seen the bus stop. I've taken a little detour down to the cliffs and managed to lose the dog by leaving him playing fetch-the-pebble in the dunes with a load of tourist kids and I've stuffed the new lead Nan bought him behind a rock and my cornrows with the green twine are holding up well under the force nine gale blowing between the houses, so I'm feeling pretty good and no one's taking any notice of me apart from some old geezer fiddling about with a spade who nods, but I ignore him, feeling his eyes following me down the street. The seagulls are screaming their heads off and swooping down to attack a waste bin outside the post office. Some little local kids are throwing stones. This passes for entertainment, presumably.

I'm not sure the bus timetable pinned to the pole is up to date, but if it is then the bus isn't coming for twenty minutes. I check the sea. Tide is well out. I sit myself down on a low wall opposite the bus stop to wait, banging my feet against the strange flat stones. The bloke with the spade is heading away up towards the castle. He has very brown arms, the colour you see on those men who spend all day digging up motorways. I'm very white. I never go in the sun and I think women like my mum who are forever holding their faces up to the light and slapping on the low factor and rushing to sit in little patches of sunshine just so they can look like they've spent the afternoon in a fucking tanning parlour, they make me sick. Brown is beautiful, is it? Only if you're white, apparently. Anyway, there never seems any point in trying to be brown when all my best mates are really black, that lovely glossy black, only their palms my colour when they hold them up, which they do often when they laugh, which is also often. Oombe laughs all the time. Laughed. I don't know why, never struck me they had much to laugh at, what with the civil war and worrying about their relatives and her knowing her uncle had died in a hail of bullets. I look at my white hands and my chewed nails. They seemed to fit in Tottenham. My white hand, Oombe's black, together, clutching at each other as we practised stupid dances down by the washing lines, *step together step together turn and bump*.

I decide I might as well spend some of my hard-earned cash on some cigs, so I get off the wall and head for the post office. There's an old woman behind the counter, serving three boys. She's weighing out some spuds into a metal cradle, fiddling about with old weights. The boys – all spotty-looking prats – are embarrassed to see me in there and start trying to be cool, no eye contact, loud conversations with each other about the chances of Newcastle next season or some such. They hold no fear for me. Boys. I look them up and down while I wait and the old woman pisses about putting their potatoes in a brown paper bag, old hands trembling, freckled and muddy. The tallest one, Baz, obviously thinks he's some kind of bossman over the others, although amid all the horseplay and snorting and whispering it's a bit hard to tell. He keeps sliding his eyes towards me and then whipping them away when he sees I haven't shifted my gaze. Long, thin, dark eyes in a long pasty face, with sunbleached hair dragged back in a ponytail, sawn-off jeans and a pretend Calvin Klein t-shirt with CK in huge letters on his puny chest. I expect this passes for high fashion in this neck of the woods. I know exactly what he's thinking. The other two seem younger, still at that you-punch-me-I'll-punch-you, wanking-every-night-but-terrified-of-the-real-thing stage. One of them's got a horrible case of acne sweeping up from his neck in a red, angry onslaught. The other one's one of those boys who's too skinny and young for his age and tries to make up for it by being funny, only he isn't. He jiggles about in his sad little stripy top telling the other ones jokes and falling about laughing, *man knocks on the door and says I'm collecting for the local swimming-pool, so the woman gives him a bucket of water, har har* . . .The other two look at me to see if I'm going to laugh or smile or something so I keep my face rigid and examine a shelf full of shoelaces and dogfood. They leave the shop noisily, the tall one finally summoning up the guts to stare at me full on, but I just stare back, expressionless, and he backs away out of the door. I can hear them honking away in the road and jostling for a quick look at me through the post-office window, squinting through the faded signs for Bisto and Camp Coffee that have probably been there since before the war, while I ask the woman for twenty Embassy and she says you don't look old enough to me and I say I'm sixteen and she says aren't you the grandchild of Mrs Weatherson at number thirty-seven, the B & B, and I say yes why don't you nip down the road and ask her how old I am if you don't believe me and I jut my chin out and raise my eyebrow and look as challenging as possible given the circumstances and she gets flustered and hands over the fags saying she doesn't want to fall out with my granny, she's a force to be reckoned with at the best of times and I hand over the dosh and I'm out of there before she changes her mind.

The boys are still hanging about, they've abandoned their tragic little string bag full of potatoes and other goodies, dumped it down on the side of the road because none of them wants to be seen with it when a girl comes along, particularly not this girl with her green braids and her leather jacket and her extremely short skirt and white white legs and boots with the buckles and straps, not like any girl they've ever seen, that's for sure.

"You lost something?" the tall one, Baz, asks me, pretending to be bold. I don't respond. I walk past them, back to my old spot by the bus stop, tearing the cellophane off the fags and dropping the paper in the road as I pass.

Round one to me.

"Only if you had a motor bike, someone's stolen it!" he yells after me. The other two explode into hysterical laughter, as though this bloke's Harry Enfield or someone.

I presume he's referring to my bikers' jacket. Normally I'd be dying, because it's completely not a fashion item, and I can't believe my mum forced me to bring it, but I know that here in this empty place with the sea and the mud and the seagulls and the sheep and not much else it's probably considered wild and outrageous and to die for, so I settle onto the wall, light my cig and stare enigmatically in the opposite direction, towards the castle. I can see the brown-armed bloke climbing the path, spade over his shoulder. They regroup, muttering.

Round Two to me.

Finally, after much murmuring and kicking of an empty Sprite can in the road, which inspires some posh woman to stop her car and tell them to kindly clear up their rubbish, they're guests on the island and should respect the environment (Round Three to me), the tall one crosses over and stands in front of me, while the other two watch, snickering, leaning on the sign for Walls Ice Cream which creaks away in the wind by the post-office entrance.

"You on holiday?" he asks.

I blow smoke in a nice straight plume into the bright sunny afternoon air, and remain silent. I know he can't leave it, because he's got those two dwarves to control, he's got to stay in charge or he's lost them. I know about boys.

"You deaf?"

I still don't answer, and take another draw on my cig.

"You got one of those for me?"

The two boys opposite are silent now, staring, waiting for something to happen. I look at the ground near the tall one's feet, keeping my face a blank. I'm having a little think, wondering if these three oiks can be of any use, but I can't think how they could be, not under any circumstances, and anyway, this one would be wanting to get his slimy teenage hand in my knickers if I so much as gave him the time of day. No, the silent treatment is the best approach, I decide.

"You know something?" he says finally. I can see he's trembling, beginning to be humiliated, deciding aggression is the better part of valour. "You're an ugly little tart, whoever you are. Cunt as wide as the Grand Canyon. I could probably shove my shopping in there and there'd still be room for a horse and cart to carry it home." He turns, grinning, to the other two for approval. They laugh, a bit uncertain. This isn't really their kind of territory. The one called Baz turns back to me, to see if I'm going to react. I look at him. Actually that was quite imaginative for a northern oik. I take another puff of cig and stare into the distance.

"She *is* deaf," he tells the others. "Or just completely thick."

"Or both," one of the others suggests, helpful.

"She's got garden twine in her hair," the sad little skinny joker suddenly says. "Fucking garden twine."

Baz latches onto this and bursts into a gale of false,

loud laughter. "Garden twine! Let's have a look –" and suddenly he's right up close poking at my hair and I pull away and he tries to grab at my crotch under my skirt only I stop him and give him a knee as close to his dick as I can get and he backs away, blinking in a bit of pain, I definitely made a connection there, and he's pretending to find it all extremely amusing and keeps saying "Green fucking garden twine!" and at the same time he's ushering the other two away down the road, laughing all the time, and giving the Sprite can a final kick against the post-office door.

The old woman from the post office comes out and stands in the street with her hands on her hips, watching them as they monkey about on the road, doing V-signs at her and shouting about garden twine and the size of my cunt. Finally she picks up the can and drops it in the waste bin, then she turns and looks at me, eyes screwed up against the sun.

"Don't let them get to you, hinny," she says.

"They haven't got to me," I say. Fucking hinny.

"Work experience up at the Donald farm," she says. "For the shearing. Although why on earth the Donalds agreed to let those little criminals loose on their livestock is a mystery to me." She notices the abandoned string bag by the side of the road and picks it up, retrieving a few potatoes that have strayed into the grass verge.

"Bus is coming," she says, and she's gone, and then the bus is definitely coming, and this is it, I can get off the fucking island at last. I see it in the distance, making slow progress along the flat, snaking road and my heart lifts, but then at exactly the moment that I'm seeing the bus and feeling happy, I suddenly see old Nanbread emerging from number thirty-seven with something under her arm, and she's got her head turned in the direction of the bus and then she's got her head turned towards me and she's registering me sitting there and she's coming towards me, and I can hear the bus engine getting louder and I'm beginning to panic a bit.

She comes right up to me.

"I thought you had the dog with you," she says.

"Nah."

"Going to do a bit of shopping in Berwick?" she asks me, eyes blue calm in her wrinkled face. I don't answer. She looks back at the approaching bus, which is now only two turns of the road away, and unrolls a bundle of paper she's carrying. "Look," she says. "What do you think?"

It says, "Stop The Development Now. Say No To Verbena". I look at her. Why is she showing me this, like we've been doing some fucking school project together, or something?

"It's for the post-office window," she says. "And one for the Church vestry." The bus is coming and she's burbling on about making boards and sticking them to lampposts and what do I think can I help her, and then the bus has pulled up, and it's the same grizzly old git of a driver who brought us to the island. The bus gives off a hot engine smell, and as the tourists pile off he's pulling hard on the handbrake so it squeals, and then he's slowly descending, stiff from the drive, and standing there with me and Nan.

"So. It's the smoker," he says. He and Nan are looking at each other as though he's said something extremely earth-shattering and significant.

Nan seems suddenly to get all brisk. "Going to Berwick to do a bit of sightseeing," she says. "Do her good. She's bored silly here. See her safely back on the six o'clock, will you, Billy?" She's giving him that significant look again. "You *are* going to be doing the six o'clock, are you?"

"I am," he says. There's a small moment while he flexes his fingers and I hear the bones crack. Then: "Right, missus." He means me. "On you get."

He climbs back on. I hesitate. Nan is rooting about in her apron pocket and suddenly, astonishingly, she's handing me a fiver. "Buy yourself a record," she says. "There's a record player in the attic. And I'll see you back here for your tea, pet."

I get on the bus and go to the back.

"No smoking!" Billy shouts from the front, and the bus jolts forward, me being its only passenger. Nan is still standing by the grass verge. Pet. I look out of the back window as she recedes in the dust, a small, tense figure. Buy yourself a record . . . !

* * *

The word that comes to mind is grey. Berwick is grey. And white. All white faces, very peculiar. The bus chugs through the main streets and I stare out at the shops, same ones as Tottenham, B&Q with a big car park and a Sainsburys and then a High Street with WH Smith and Abbey National and Marks & Spencers and Nationwide and Midland Bank and River Island and Boots and Dolcis and the NatWest and McDonalds. Just like home, really, except for the grey brick and the white faces. Scott Walker keeps drifting into my brain. The love of her life. The real love.

Billy stops the bus in a bay at the bus station and turns the engine off. "End of the line," he says, his eyes meeting mine in his mirror. "See you back here at six."

Not if I see you first.

"If you miss the bus you've missed the island," he says. "High tide's at six thirty." I swing up the aisle and jump off, ignoring him. I'll decide my own timetable, thank-you very much, Wrinkly Brigade.

"That'll be seventy pee," he says. Shit. I climb back on and count out the money, slapping the coins down on the little black plastic dish. He takes the money and issues me a ticket from his machine. I take it, and as I turn to get off, I make sure he sees me drop it on the steps of his precious bus. I wait for him to shout. He doesn't. I walk away.

"Get her," says a bloke behind a newspaper stand as I pass. "It's Scary Spice." I think he means me.

I head off into the town and wander about for a bit. I manage to lift some blue glittery nail varnish from SupaDrug and go out into the sunshine again to find a resting-place. I position myself on a wooden bench going round a tree growing out of the concrete in some shopping precinct, pull off my boots and do my toenails carefully with the blue. There's already chipped maroon, and I should have nicked some nail-polish remover and a bag of cotton wool balls, but I can't be bothered to go back in again, so I paint the blue over the maroon, doing it slowly and carefully, three coats, and pausing all the while to let the layers dry in the sun. I'm thinking about where to go next and wishing I'd at least packed some kind of bag.

There's a pub opposite the bench, with tables outside and people pretending they're in the South of France, downing their pints and trying to look sophisticated which is a bit difficult when you're wearing a shellsuit and a baseball hat with a plastic picture of Yogi bear on the front and your wife's fat with great ponds of underarm sweat seeping through her polyester sundress and the kid in the pushchair's grizzling and getting a smack because it's just tipped all its barbecue-flavoured crisps all over the pavement. Still, it gives me some entertainment, watching the comings and goings as I do my toenails and try to make a decision about where to go. I can't go back to London. Oombe's dad wouldn't let me stay with them, and I don't want to go to any of the other girls. They'll take the piss and ask me questions and stare at me funny and whisper about me when I'm not there, and their mothers will be wanting to ring up my mum and then the Welfare will show up and I'd be totally ashamed, because the Welfare is who shows up when your life is completely rubbish, and you become a social outcast and have to eat your dinner on your own. And at MLK, once you get to that point, there's no going back. You either have to hang about with all the other divs and failures, or you kill yourself. Like Lorna McKenzie. That's what we heard. After she left the school. Lorna McKenzie with the schizophrenic mum and the brother in a special school and no dad to speak of and peculiar jumpers that sagged at the bottom. Is no more.

"Wey-ey." Someone's come and sat down next to me while I'm thinking about Lorna McKenzie, and I don't look round, because I know it's some northern geezer, they all say "wey-ey" which I think is like wotcha. I don't answer. I'm aware of him, though. He's a runty little bloke in those pretend Nike running trousers and a vest, wiry brown muscles and a gold crucifix glinting. Big new trainers. "Nice colour." He's referring to my toes. Says *cooler*. I wait to see what he wants. They always want something.

"Like a drink?" He pauses. "We could sit outside, at one of them tables. Or else I could bring it over here."

"I'm too young."

He's looking at me, surprised. "Too young? You're kidding me. Seventeen, I'd have said. Seventeen or eighteen."

I don't answer. I could kill for a can of Coke.

"What's that called, that colour?" *Cooler* again.

"Starlight."

"Nice."

There's a silence, almost companionable. He's no threat.

I decide there's no harm in it.

"A can of Coke would be nice."

He gets up and grins at me. He's got an ugly thin little face and a black space where one of his front teeth should be. "Don't go away." I wasn't intending to. He disappears into the pub, and before I've finished the final coat of Starlight he's back, with a pint for himself and a can for me. Gentlemanly, he pulls the ring tab off and hands me the can. It's beautifully cold, and I drink a lot, very slowly, feeling the fiery fizz slide down my throat, warming as it descends.

"You from London, then?"

"Yup."

"Holiday?"

"Nope."

"What – you live here? Berwick?" he says this disbelievingly, as though I'm Madonna or someone. He shakes his head, sipping at his pint, then wiping away the little foam moustache on his upper lip with the back of his brown thin hand. I notice a fistful of silver rings.

"Holy Island," I say, unable to keep just a little lilt of pride out of my tone. After all, the island's got to have a bit more class than this dump, even to oiks like him.

Now he's doing major acting, mega-shocked. "You?" He says. "*You?* Holy Island?" He lets out a low whistle. "I bet you get them all on the alert in the Red Lion." He laughs to himself, amused at the thought. "Full to attention . . ."

He's looking at me sideways. "And what do you do for entertainment on Holy Island, then?"

I shrug. "Nothing. What the fuck is there to do?"

I can feel him watching me as he drinks, assessing, making some kind of a decision. Finally he says, "Want a bit of puff?" Only he says *poof* and for a moment I'm confused – is this him thinking I want to fuck some queer bloke, or what? I have visions of stranger sex than I want to deal with, threesomes and me somehow trapped in the middle, then I realise he means blow, and I smile at him. I'm desperate. No drugs since that *khat* on the bus and the little joint before the island, and that feels like years ago. I know Mum's probably got a little lump of dope stashed somewhere, but there's something about sharing drugs with your mother that is just too disgusting, so I haven't even bothered to look.

"What do I have to do for it?" I ask.

He looks a bit thunderstruck. "Do?" I wait. Then suddenly, unexpectedly, he gives a funny little surprised laugh. "You don't have to do anything, hen. I was just being sociable." He takes another swig of his pint. "It's in my house. Just down the street."

I nod. "Right. And all I have to do is come there with you, give you a quickie and the blow's mine, right?"

He looks at me, and I can't work out what's going on with his face. He seems genuinely gobsmacked. "Suit yerself," he says, and gets up and walks away. So I follow him and say no, no, sorry, I misunderstood, didn't mean to offend, yes please, should we go now? And then he's walking back to the bench finishing his pint and I'm stuffing my boots back on and screwing the lid on the pot of Starlight and we're walking away down the precinct and into the shadow of an alleyway by the side of Toys'R'Us and I'm following him round a multi-storey car park making small talk about what music I like though of course he's never heard of anyone from Africa so that's a bit of a dead end, particularly as he's keen on REM, and there's the back entrance to a row of new flats and we go up a fire escape and onto a concrete landing and he makes me wait at the door, which is a bit of a surprise and he goes in and comes out with two skinny spliffs.

"Here you are," he says. "Free, gratis and for nothing. Enjoy."

I thank him and walk away, still not quite sure if this is really happening, and then he suddenly calls out

"Next time you're passing . . . – ask for Charlie Heaton. Always welcome."

I turn to look at him, and he's leaning in the doorway, grinning. "Only next time," he says, "I might ask for a little payment."

Fair enough. I walk away, feeling pleased. Two spliffs

and no donging of the big stick in any shape or form. Good deal.

Only now I don't know what to do. I walk about a bit, only the shops are closing and as the shadows get longer on the pavement people are going home, loaded down with their BHS carrier bags and their hot toddlers, traffic jam in the main street and drivers with the windows rolled down, shirt-sleeved and shouting at their passengers and at each other. I find myself heading back the way I came.

Billy's sitting in a shadowy part of a bus bay, smoking a fag, reading a paper with *Morning Star* across the front. He doesn't say anything, just looks at me. I walk past, trying to make out I'm heading off somewhere and just happen to be taking a short cut through the bus station, and he suddenly says, "It's Bay Five. Door's open."

And I'm walking, very slowly in the drooping heat of the afternoon, with the sun low beyond the flat grey of the buildings, and I've decided that I'm going back.

All right. I know I said I was going. But I've run through the options and there aren't any. I know I should be feeling defeated, but I get on the bus and go to the back, past the murmuring people with their bags and their kids and their stares and their nudgings, and I settle in my same seat, and I feel the two spliffs in my jacket pocket, and I feel okay.

The thing is, although I've tried hard not to think about it, I know that something's been lurking in my head all day. Something that pushed all the other thoughts away, which is a good thing, because the stuff inside my head is not happy stuff and anyway I don't want to think about all that. It's that picture Mum had. The eyes. That mouth. Something in there speaks to me and I've been carrying it around since I got on the bus, hardly knowing that I was.

We're connected, me and him, but I don't know how. He's the reason I am who I am, according to Nanbread. Me. Joanna. I am Joanna because of him. Perhaps I'm not French at all. Perhaps it's all been a great big fucking lie.

Billy climbs on the bus and shouts a loud Geordie greeting to various people and then the bus starts up and there's a sudden blast of heat as the automatic door hisses and shuts, and the bus moves slowly away and out of the bus bay and it's too late to get off now even if I *did* change my mind, but I don't and I haven't. I'm going back to Holy Island, to find out about my mum and Scott Walker.

Chapter Four

Where hes te been, my canny hinny?
An'where hes te been, my bonny bairn?
Aw was up an' doon, seekin' my hinny;
Aw was throo' the toon, seekin' for my bairn.

From Songs of Northern England

"This is ridiculous," I said to Billy. We were lying in the old barn beyond the Big Field, on some sacks behind the rusting hulk of the Donalds' old tractor.

He grinned. "Like being a lad again," he said, propped up on one elbow and looking at me, his eyes crinkling at the corners. It was the eyes that got me, that first time on the bus. Cath would have said it was like Clark Gable grinning at Claudette Colbert in *It Happened One Night*. All I knew is they were bright blue.

I never thought the day would come. Creeping about

89

in a barn, sex with my clothes on, Billy's hands excited like never before. Perhaps it's the fear of someone coming by – although the likelihood of that is about nil. You don't battle into the teeth of the wind across the Big Field unless you've got a reason. Even the sheep stay over by the road, pressed against the hedge.

I sat up, and began to button my blouse. He put his hand on me and said, "It's early yet."

I pushed him away, struggling not to feel grubby and ashamed, like a teenage girl who has done something she shouldn't in a back alley. Billy and me in the comfort of my house – that's a different thing. With the curtains drawn and the telly on and no one to know or care what we get up to. My family have done this to me. "I'd better get back," I said.

He stood up and began slowly brushing straw from his trousers. "I could kill those two," he said. "Especially that little tart. You know she broke into one of the castle sheds? The warden chucked her out. She was smoking, of course. Called him every bad word in the English language, by all accounts – some he'd never heard before – and he's a chap with a tongue on him. They had to buy a new padlock."

I suppose he had reason to dislike Joanna. After all, he watched her comings and goings, knew what she was up to. I suppose I'm more liberal than Billy. She's just a bairn, I kept telling him. She's playing with fire, like all teenagers. She'll be all right. She's worldly wise, that one.

Billy had been playing detective. He often drove her on the bus across the causeway and one day he followed her, out of the bus station, shadowing her on the streets of Berwick like Bergerac. That's when he found out. Joanna was seeing some married man in the town, and he was supplying her with marijuana. She'd come out of the house smoking it, bold as brass, as if she wanted to be arrested. Billy came back and told me, announcing it with the air of someone who has just dug up a body in the herbaceous border. I suppose I should have been shocked, but I remember marijuana from the Yanks in the war. It didn't seem to do anyone much harm. But I was worried by the thought of her and this married man. I know we were all at it in my day (and some of us still are), but not at fourteen. I had already caught her getting up to what looked like no good with that snake in the suit from Verbena Hotels. I threw him out and gave her the benefit of the doubt, but she was up to something. I dare not think what was going on there. I was scared for Joanna about the sex, if that's what she was doing. Surely not, not at fourteen? I left some condoms by her bed, just in case. She never mentioned them to me, but she never threw them back in my face either.

What about all the bus fares to Berwick? Where was that money coming from?

She wouldn't go to school. I kept telling Cath we should be organising something for the autumn term, but she was just quietly boozing herself to death and not interested. I broached the subject with Joanna and she went berserk. Said I could do what I liked, but she wouldn't go. So I've dropped it for the moment. Why should I have sleepless nights over the education of a mouthy little madam who would steal from my purse every day if I hadn't learned my lesson and now kept it locked in the pantry? Which again raised the question of bus fares. She wasn't stealing from me. Cath had no money I knew, because she was borrowing from me for the booze. Joanna got money from somewhere, but the where didn't bear thinking about. None of my business anyway.

I was adjusting my tights, pulling up the wrinkles round the knees and humming to myself. Billy stopped plucking the straw out of his turn-ups and looked at me.

"What's that?" he asked. "That song?"

I cursed to myself. I was getting as mad as them. "It's called 'The Sun Ain't Gonna Shine Any More'," I said.

Billy frowned. "Doesn't ring a bell."

"It wouldn't."

"It's not Paul Robeson, is it?"

I shook my head angrily. "Bloody Scott Walker."

"Never heard of him. And what are you doing, swearing, bonny lass? Since when did you swear?"

As we made our way across the Big Field, heads bowed against the wind, kittiwakes wheeling overhead, I told him about Scott Walker. About how Joanna had taken to sitting up in the attic playing all the old records belonging to her mam, about how I'd gone up there and found her pinning up all the old pictures – that face – those brown eyes, that weak boy's mouth, that great mass of blond hair – for how many years had I lived with that face, and now here it was back to haunt me. The house rang with the sound of his voice, the brooding lyrics of his blasted songs, the gloomy depressing presence of him, Mr Scott Tragedy Walker.

"I don't understand," Billy shouted above the wind. "What is it you've got against him?"

I couldn't tell him. It was all too long ago and far away. I yelled that I'd had it all once before, with Cath when she was a teenager, and I just didn't want to go through it all again. I heard the lameness of what I said being carried away across the pasture, and Billy only half-hearing my answer.

We paused at the sheep-pen.

"Better split up here," I said.

He gave me a smile, but I could see the hurt. "Like a couple of spies," he said. This was an argument we had already had and he'd lost. Why, he'd said, why can't I be seen with you? Are you ashamed? I couldn't tell him that it would be a betrayal of Tommy, could I? All the islanders seeing me with another man, when half of them had been at Tommy's funeral. Sometimes I wish we lived on the other side of the world, where no one would know or care about your business.

I'm not saying Tommy would mind me having a

LILIE FERRARI

sweetheart. After all, I've been alone for more than thirty years. It's not Tommy, really. It's me. Already I could feel the list of chores crowding in, obliterating Billy and our randy half-hour behind the tractor. I was going to make a pot pie but I hadn't checked if I had enough suet. I needed to get down the garden and pick beans before it got dark. And I should have cranked up the stove a good hour ago, to prepare for baking. Plus I knew that the dog would be stuck inside waiting for me, since no one else cared whether it lived or died. Not that I did. I'm not a dog person, me. But it was a living creature and deserved some kind of a life, not the continual attempts at murder perpetrated on it by my grandchild, who locked it in sheds, left it on the beach, dropped it in the burn, never fed it, never looked at it, and only made contact when her boot felt like kicking something. She's a devil, that one. It must be that French blood.

Billy tried to kiss me as we parted, but I turned my face away so his lips were planted on my cold cheek. It wasn't an unkind impulse, just my brain somewhere down in the vegetable patch and our stolen time now just a memory, a silly thing we shouldn't have done. I couldn't help it. I did feel grubby now.

I stood and watched him head back across the field to where his bus stood idle on the road beyond. No one would think anything of it – Billy always parked the bus there on this shift, it was a familiar sight. He was a few years younger than me, but in the failing light he seemed

94

suddenly very old, body bent forward propelled by the wind like a leaf. This man had had his hands on me and I had liked it, there was no getting away from it. All those years since I let a man touch me, and now I remembered what pleasure it could bring; but the hands were gnarled. The flesh that they traced patterns on was wrinkled. Perhaps it had all come too late.

I walked home angry, wishing Cath would pack her bags, take her brat and go, tired of their intrusive presence in my house, their clothes on the washing-line, their voices on the stairs, Cath and her interminable drinking and her frowsy hair, Joanna a shadow always leaving, or about to leave, or an absence, just the mournful baritone of Scott Walker seeping through the floorboards to tell me when she was in. And the dog, of course, always waiting in the hall, waiting to flick its pathetic tail at me whenever I appeared, its eyes annoyingly hopeful. I wanted to get it by the throat and say – don't expect a thing from me, lad – I've nothing to give.

As I turned into my gate, I looked back at the castle, don't ask me why, and saw Joanna, silhouetted dark against the sky, standing on the dry stone wall of the castle garden up on the hill, away from the great dark battlements and towering walls. She was just standing. I could tell it was her, all that rat's-tail hair blowing about. She didn't move. I wondered what she was up to. She didn't strike me as the type to be interested in a historical garden. Tourists go up there. Perhaps she was messing about with those boys doing work experience on the Donalds' farm. Jessie at the post office told me she had seen them together several times, although she had the impression they were bullying Joanna, which made me laugh.

"I doubt it," I said. "If ever there was a bully, she's it. I can't see those skinny lads getting the better of that young madam."

Jessie, busy unpacking tins of baked beans onto the back shelf, gave me one of her looks. She was wondering why I was so nasty about my grandchild. Jessie has six of them, and knows their birthdays off by heart, talks about them as if they were here yesterday, and has a row of those school photographs – the ones where they sit scrubbed and smiling against a blue background – on display above the grille of the post-office counter, like big game trophies. We're not exactly sisters under the skin, me and Jessie, even though she lets me put up my posters. She's a WI woman.

Cath had started on the booze already, sitting by the unlit grate in the living-room, flicking cigarette ash into the hearth, glass in hand. What could I say? It was her business if she wanted to drink herself into an early grave. She didn't even look up. I could hear the puppy yelping. She'd shut it in the kitchen again, which is what she had taken to doing if I was out.

"I thought you were in the garden," she said.

I didn't answer. I went out into the hall and down the

passage to the kitchen. The dog was right behind the door and as I opened it he burst through and almost knocked me down. The size of his paws worried me. He was going to be a big dog. I fetched the ingredients from the pantry. I had just enough suet. How on earth were they going to look after that beast when they went back to London? Assuming they were going back.

Cath had followed me carrying her glass, and now she sat at the table, watching me as I mixed the flour and suet in the big earthenware bowl.

"Don't you weigh anything?" she asked.

"No need. I've been making this all my life. I know what six ounces of flour looks like," I said.

I felt her eyes studying me as I floured the board and began to roll the dough.

"If you want to help," I said, trying not to sound irritated and failing, "you could be cutting up the meat."

She shuddered. "No, thanks. Couldn't it just be vegetables this time?"

Ruddy vegetarians. "No," I said, stalking to the pantry, "No, it couldn't. You'll just have to have mash and a side vegetable."

"Joanna won't eat that."

"She ate it all right the other day," I said, hearing the note of triumph I couldn't quite suppress. Another nail in Cath's trendy coffin. They had told me they didn't eat meat, but within a day of smelling my baking Joanna had somehow overcome her city scruples and was tucking into bacon, sausages, steak and kidney – all the flesh I could offer her. I know it was mean. I was undermining her mother. But she needed fattening up, poor sad skinny girl. And anyway, it's a silly fad, all this weeping and wailing over animals. That Linda McCartney's got a lot to answer for.

The front door crashed, and the puppy gave a muffled yelp from the corridor. Joanna came in, pink-faced from the wind, hair like a haystack, long jumper sleeves dangling below the cuffs of her leather jacket. She crossed the kitchen and helped herself to a cigarette from her mother's packet.

"At the booze already?" she said to Cath, disgusted.

"Hey, you – not in my kitchen," I said sharply. "You want to smoke, you leave my house."

Sighing, she threw the cigarette down on the table. She was always surprising me, this girl. I never expected her to listen to me, to take any notice when I laid down the law, but oddly, she did.

She flopped into a chair opposite her mother.

"Where have you been?" I asked, pretending to be more interested in slicing up the lumps of steak.

"Nowhere," she said. There was a silence, broken only by the rasping, desperate sound of Cath inhaling on her cigarette, eyes glazing into the distance, miles away as usual. Joanna was staring at her. I could almost see all the little cogs and wheels in her brain working.

"So did you ever meet him?" she asked.

Cath dragged herself back from wherever she had been. With that Frenchman, probably. "Who?"

"Scott Walker. Did you ever go to a concert? See him sing?"

I got busy with the kidneys, struggling not to say something sarcastic. Instead I listened, curious to hear what Cath would say about that time in her life.

She gulped at her Scotch and then put the glass back on the table. "No, I never met him. You didn't meet Scott Walker. He was absolutely unattainable."

Not for want of trying, though. No. I tossed the meat in the flour and seasoning. I must not speak.

"You could have stood at the stage door, or something." Joanna's face was intense, as if this was the most important thing in the world. I know teenage girls have fantasies – mine was Spencer Tracy – but for a man who would by now be old enough to be her father, Joanna's obsession seemed distorted, perverse.

Cath shot a look at me but I looked away. Time to start rolling out the lid of the pot pie. I sprinkled more flour on the board.

"I saw him," Cath said.

Joanna perked up. "When?"

"I was a student. In London."

"Nineteen sixty-six," I said, unable to keep quiet any longer. How could I forget? It was the year she spoiled everything, crushed my dreams, all the bright ideas I had about one of my children doing the things I'd never got to do. And Cathy was going to do them for me. Until she saw Scott Walker.

Cath didn't look at me. "Nineteen sixty-six. I was nineteen."

"You went to a concert?"

Cath laughed, a short, angry laugh. "I went to hundreds of concerts."

"Twenty-fifth of March, nineteen sixty-six," I couldn't resist saying, as I rolled the dough into a fat circle on the board. "Finsbury Park Astoria. That was the first time."

Joanna was looking at me, open-mouthed. "How do you know that?"

"Because I bought her the ticket. As a birthday present," I said. The dough was now thin, with a floury sheen. I draped it over the rolling-pin and laid it across the pie dish, allowing the edges to droop over the side.

Foolish me. I bought her the ticket because her letters home had been full of Scott Walker, how much she loved him, how the sound of his voice stopped her feeling homesick for Northumberland, how he was nothing like the pimply boys at the university, how she could tell he had a soul, that he felt things, that he was a gentle human being, not like the loud and confident lads in the common room at the university, shouting over their copies of *Marxism Today* and *International Times*, wanting you to be what they wanted you to be, not what you really were. A bit like you, Mam, she wrote. A bit like you.

I spun the bowl around, slicing off the spare dough looping round the rim. Cath got up and poured herself another drink. "Roy Orbison was top of the bill," she said. "And Lulu . . . But we were all there to see the Walker Brothers, really. I don't even remember the others – what they sang, how they looked . . . "

"And how did *he* look?" Again, that bright, desperate look from Joanna, her body tense, leaning forward, watching her mother.

Cath sat, deflating slowly. Her eyes took on that distant look again. She didn't seem to be aware that she was talking to Joanna. "He was the most beautiful man I've ever seen," she said.

Joanna was silent for a moment, absorbing this, nodding solemnly in agreement. But she was not satisfied. "What about – other times?" she said. "Did you ever see him when he wasn't on stage? In the street? Outside the theatre?"

Cath smiled. "St John's Wood. We tracked him there, to his flat. Went round all the newsagents till we found one who delivered his papers. He moved soon after that." She began to trace one of her sad circles on the table. "Then he went to a place on the Fulham Road. That one was harder. But we found him in the end."

Joanna was agape. "You found him? What do you mean? What did he say?"

He didn't say anything, foolish girl. He ran.

Cath had not heard the questions. She smiled to

herself. And for a moment I saw the sad and silly smile of that nineteen-year-old girl as I tried to talk some sense into her all those years ago. I took the day off work, said it was a family emergency, but they still docked my pay at the factory. Coach to Newcastle, then the train to London. I sat in her student room, amid the packed suitcases and the abandoned textbooks and I pleaded with her to stay, clutching at her hand. Think of your future, girl. All that education going to waste. You're a bright lass, don't throw it away, not for the sake of some silly pop star, he'll be forgotten in a few years and you'll have your life ahead of you. Not many girls get where you've got. The London School of Economics! Trade Union history! The real world, our country's backbone, the root and branch of our lives, not some stupid Yank with a pretty face and a good baritone. Don't walk away from all this. Don't. Please. For my sake. For your mam. And all she said was: "You smell of fish. All this way to see me and you still smell of fish."

I had finished folding the greaseproof paper round the rim, even though my hands were trembling. The crash of the oven door as I slammed it shut, pie safely inside, made them look at me. Two faces, so different, yet connecting to me. Cath seemed to wake up.

"I followed him everywhere," she told Joanna. "For months. A year. No – more than that."

I could see she was doing the same sum in her head that I was doing, although I was pretending to be busy wiping my hands on a dishcloth and clearing up. Our eyes met.

"Until nineteen sixty-eight," I said. "March."

"How did you live? How could you afford to do that?"

"Her grant. For the university. She spent her grant money." I heard my voice as if someone else was speaking, harsh, dry.

That chewed finger tracing those never-ending circles on the table top slowed to a standstill.

"Why did you stop? Mum?" Joanna's impatience unnerved me. I had not seen her passionate about anything before.

"The Walker Brothers broke up," Cath said dully. "Scott didn't want to do it any more."

And by March you were in Ward Seventeen, Friern Barnet, broke and so full of largactyl you couldn't speak. In the loony bin.

Joanna hadn't finished. "But what about later?" She persisted. "Years later? Did you see him again? What happened to him? Where did he go? What did you do? Did you –"

Cath's glass landed with an unsteady crash on the table, and she stood up suddenly. She lowered her head, as if the sudden movement had made her head swim. "No," she said. "No. Shut up. No more bloody questions. Scott Walker broke them up. Didn't want fans. Didn't want to sing any more. Not with the other two."

She walked unsteadily to the door. The dog looked up,

hopeful, then subsided again. He had learned already that Cath wasn't good for anything much. She turned in the doorway, holding on to the brass handle for support. "Sang on his own for a while. Made these funny obscure records. Then disappeared completely." She turned and headed away into the gloom of the corridor. We listened as she made her unwieldy way up the stairs. "Off the face of the earth . . ." We heard her say. "Shut up. Don't want to talk about it . . ."

There was silence. Joanna had not moved. Her eyes were on me, as if expecting me to clarify things, fill in the gaps. I took my bowl full of flour-caked utensils over to the sink and dropped them in with a crash. "Don't look at me," I said. I began to run the tap, grateful for the noise of water gushing into the bowl, glad my back was turned so she couldn't see the beginnings of tears as I tried to shake off the memories. She said nothing.

While I washed the dishes and dried them, stacked them in the cupboard, checked the pie, put the plates in to warm, put the kettle on, got out the jar of custard powder ready for the pudding, she said nothing. Finally I turned to look at her. She was sitting in exactly the same place, still facing where her mother had sat, but now her head was turned away and she was staring out of the window, although there was nothing much to see apart from the dustbin, the compost heap and the old outdoor lav.

"What did you do today?" I asked her.

She did not move. I wondered if she was crying.

"I saw you up at the castle garden," I said. "Were you with those boys from the farm? The boys from Donalds'?"

Still no answer. "You were on the garden wall," I said. "The castle garden. Were you playing a game with them?"

Her cold, hard little face turned to me then. "I wouldn't touch them with a bargepole. There was a bloke there," she said.

"A bloke?"

"A gardener."

"That'll be Jack. Was he a Yank?"

"Dunno."

"He's all right. Quiet type. No harm."

She got up. "He told me to piss off."

I smiled to myself. Met someone as rude as you, young madam.

She was going to go to the attic again, I knew, and sit listening to Scott Walker, staring at the face on the wall, lost in the same dreams that had led her mother so far from the straight and narrow that she'd never managed to clamber back.

I heard her feet clacking on the tiles in the hall, that boot buckle still loose, then a door slammed.

"Tea at seven!" I yelled, but I doubt she heard me.

The phone rang. I went out to answer it, saying "Marygate Guest House" automatically, and picking up a pencil. The only people who ever phoned were people who had seen my number in the *Golden Coast and Islands of Northumberland Guide Book.* But the voice on the other end was French, and I knew immediately who it was.

"Sylvie?" He said, uncertain. He said my name the French way, prettily. "I'm wondering if Cathy is there –" I went cold. He began speaking rapidly, to cover his embarrassment. "Cathy – your daughter – you remember me? Your son-in-law – Gabriel Lefèvre – I know it's been years – I'm just wondering if Cathy is there –"

Before I had time to think, before I even had an opinion on him phoning, I heard my voice say, casual, "Good heavens, you mean you've lost my daughter?"

He said charmingly he thought she'd said she was coming on a visit, only he wasn't clear which relative, and he had a message for her from work. Did I have any idea where she was? He was a good liar. I felt a cold hand descend on my heart. I told him I hadn't heard from Cathy for a couple of years now, and no – she certainly wasn't here. Nor did I know where she could be. After promising to let him know if she showed up, and making a show of writing down his phone number, I hung up.

We ate a silent supper. I looked at my drunk daughter across the table and wondered about her and the Frenchman, but said nothing. We all went to bed early. There was nothing on telly, no one had anything to say, so it seemed like the best solution. Joanna was the last up. I left her on the front step staring out of the front door, smoking one of her mother's cigarettes (I allowed it on the doorstep), staring at the gaunt, hunched silhouette of the castle on the hill. I told her to lock up and left her to it.

I wasn't going to tell Cath about the phone call. Don't ask me why. I think I was becoming a little insane. After all, I wanted these two out of my house, and I'd just ruined the perfect opportunity to put them on the next bus off the island, bags packed, mangy dog and all. You'd think I would have had more sense.

Then the next morning, when I was laying the table (no guests again, just three places, for me and Joanna and Cath) she suddenly appeared, like a screaming banshee, red hair on end, white-lipped and howling, and she knocks me to the flagstones and she screeches that I lied to her husband, I told a lie, it was none of my business. I was cowering, arm up to protect my buzzing head where she had hit me and I wondered out loud between blows how she knew and she told me. Joanna told her. Joanna heard the phone call. Joanna told her! And all the time as I tried to get up she pushed me back down with rough hands until finally she went out and I sat too stunned to weep, bruised and rigid on the floor.

Cathy. My own daughter. Flesh of my flesh. She hit me. I'm in bed now, shaken and stirred, like a James Bond cocktail. Suddenly I feel like an old, frightened woman. Vulnerable. Suddenly I'm closer to dying than I want to be at this juncture. I've let these monsters into my house and now I'm stuck with them.

I can hear Joanna in the attic. The click of the record-player lid opening, the pause as she puts the record on the turntable, the tiny hiss before the song begins. The swoop and fullness of a string orchestra, then the dark voice, disembodied, floating down, rich and passionate.

All at once I miss you
So long since I've kissed you
How I long to look into your eyes
Yes I still dream about you
My world is lost without you
For you were my first love
And first love never ever dies . . .

Chapter Five

Yo, dude – wake up and get out of bed!

BART SIMPSON ALARM CLOCK

The dog showed up again, scratching at the back door, insanely pleased to see everyone. Nanbread looking at me sideways. What happened to that new lead I bought him? Don't say that one's gone missing as well. Don't ask me . . .

Can't go back to see Charlie in Berwick, not after last week, though that's it for dope, I don't know where else I'm going to get any. There were five blokes in his living-room, all squashed in, high as kites and watching dirty films, a lot of smoke and grinning and laughing, the kind of thing I remember from coming home and finding Dad all tanked up and excited in front of some video, waiting for me to come home and do the business. Five of them –

I think Charlie thought I was going to do it to all of them, raise his status down the Brown Bear, procurer of young girls, but I couldn't, not for a ton of blow, no way.

I was scared shitless. Sick to my stomach and quivering inside, but holding my head up, telling Charlie can't stop, Mum's waiting for me outside so he won't follow me or make me stay. He's out in the narrow passage, leaning against the wall with me trapped against it, brown sinewy arms pressed either side of my head, cig in his mouth. He's an ugly bastard and his breath stinks of hamburgers. Tells me I've got nothing to be afraid of, he'll look after me, nothing will happen I don't want to happen. He doesn't know about my dad obviously, so he doesn't know I've heard this before and I know it's all bollocks. Doesn't he realise? None of it, I want none of it to happen, I don't even want to be here in the first place and all this reasonable grown-up adult-to-adult chat is his way of making it all right in his head, not in mine.

I smile brightly and don't look in his eyes and tell him it's okay, just wanted a bit of dope to tide me over till next week. I'll be back, can't stop, Mum'll be knocking on the door in a minute if I don't leave. And there's a moment, a dark scary bottomless second when I think in a little frozen voice in my head that he isn't going to let me go, that it's going to be like Fred West and I'm going to end up in pieces in the cellar after all those sweaty belching fired-up gits in the front room have had their turn and then he smiles and I see that gap in his front teeth and he's telling me he'll see me next week then and handing me a couple of joints to be going on with and then I'm out the door and legging it through the car park like Linford Christie, imagining Charlie and his mates all plunking their twangers one more time to their dirty film, all moaning about the lack of the real thing.

So I won't go back there. Can't. Pity.

This is such an empty place. I can't explain. The bus to Berwick goes along this empty empty road, nothing but lorries heading for Scotland, fields full of sheep, enormous sky, green everywhere. And it's worse on the island. When the causeway's open there are Christians tramping about wearing cagoules and hiking boots and buying Celtic crucifixes in the shops and creeping round the red ruins of the priory with solemn Christian faces or toiling up the hill to the castle with the wind burning their faces and the gulls screaming above their heads. Car parks all full, ice-cream vans and wingeing kids, and Nan's spare rooms all full of large Americans with binoculars and no peace anywhere except the attic, where I'm living now, got Nanbread to say I could take a bed up there and me and her pushing and shoving an old fold-up bed up the stairs and nearly breaking our backs and Mum I don't know where as usual. Up here there's just me and Scott Walker and I can look out of the skylight and there's just the harbour with those blokes who fished me out of the sea doing their lobster pots and there's the field of sheep (always sheep) and beyond that the hill and the castle, standing high up above the village and the sea, and it's always where I look first when I get up, because the castle and the sky make a different picture every morning. Once I saw a double rainbow. Scott Walker staring down from the wall with dark grey eyes and two rainbows outside my window and 'The Sun Ain't Gonna Shine Any More'.

Where was I? The island. So it's like living in Disneyland when the tide's out and everyone swarms over here and people stare at you because they can see you must live here because you've got this sodding dog trailing after you wherever you go. But then the tide comes in and then it's like no other place in the world, because you are completely alone, I mean really alone, and no one can get to you or speak to you or bother you. It's like a spell. The tide comes in, the island's cut off and everyone goes to sleep. Or that's how it seems to me. Suddenly there are no cars in Marygate any more, the car parks are suddenly empty and the tourist shops pull down their shutters and the tea rooms lock their doors and Billy the busman parks by the bus stop and falls asleep over his copy of the *Morning Star* and Nan slows down and listens to her Paul Robeson records in the living-room and nods off over her afternoon cup of tea.

What do I do? I'm like in a trance as well, only I'm not one for sleeping once I've got up (about lunch-time, according to Nan) so I usually go wandering. I know the whole island now, from the Snook where a million rabbits live to the Lough where the seabirds screech and wheel all day, the wide white empty beach in Coves Bay and the black horse in the field by the church who ignores me completely when I look over the wall. It's big and small at the same time, this island. Big because you can get lost on the dunes in five minutes flat, not knowing if you're facing the sea or the village, disappearing down great valleys of sand and tearing your hands on the marram grass as you clamber up the other side, feet sinking, wind blowing and a raging sky above. Small because I know every paving stone in the village, who lives in what fucking house, which ones are the holiday lets, what the vicar said in his sermon on Sunday, how Mr Ridley's roses have got the blackspot, who went to line-dancing in the village hall on Saturday, Davy Redpath's getting a new boat, the dry stone wall at the end of Fenkle Street is falling down and they're going to repair it starting next week. On and on, every single tiny little bit of information is passed around and looked at and talked about and pondered on and passed on again. I could scream. And there's nowhere to hide. Wherever I go, I'm seen. I'll come in and Nan'll say "Jessie said she saw you down by the Pilgrim's Way writing things in the sand," or "What were you doing throwing stones at the Donalds' geese?" And all the time those work-experience fucknobs following me around, calling me a bitch and a whore. Baz, Paulie and the little one I call The Sniffer because that's what he does and he doesn't deserve to have a whole name to himself, not a proper name like a human being. It's like being back at school listening to them trailing behind me showing off. I take no notice. This makes them even angrier, but they're so busy trying to pretend they don't care when they're so horny and so desperate to get at me, being the only presentable female on the island under the age of about seventy only they can't show it because they're trapped in their desperate boys' bodies, all pimples and desperate wanking, and me, I'm the object of their sly in-the-dark moanings and spurtings and it makes them furious, which is why they are my shadows, always round the next corner or hiding in the dunes or chucking sheep-shit at me. Me and them and Mum and Nan going round and round in a windy circle, spied on by the islanders.

Mum says it's like *The Prisoner* starring Patrick McGoohan, a seminal series from the sixties, apparently. Only minus the bouncing ball. Sometimes I think she's finally gone completely mad. She's still drinking, but she's become a bit mysterious. Not in the house for most of the day and I never see her when I go on my wandering, so I don't know where she goes. Always back for the sun going over the yard-arm, though.

I've finally got rid of the dog. After all that business with Nan getting the phone call from Dad and not telling Mum and me telling Mum and Mum hitting Nan and them not speaking to each other for hours and hours. Nan shouting at me to take the dog, take the dog whenever I go out, so I take him on a bit of string and I march him over the dunes to the North Shore and I find a sort of little cave thing where the wind has hollowed out a hole in the sand, and I put him in and then I make him sit. Nan's been teaching him to stay still and not move, to stop him digging in her compost heap when she's trying to turn it, so now if you say *Stay!* in a really booming stern kind of voice he wiggles his tail a bit and waits, not moving an inch, till you tell him okay, then he leaps all over you like you've just returned from a long trip to the North Pole and back. Only this time I'm not going to say okay.

"Stay!"

He sits there, eyes bright, motionless. This is a game he likes. Nan can leave him there, desperate and surrounded by the wonderful whiffs of compost and he won't move, not even if she goes back into the house and forgets him for half an hour, which she's been known to do. I know he'll do it for me, because he's my little slave, even though I don't want one.

So he sits there, panting a bit, eager, and I turn away, no looking back or I'm done for and then I run like a lunatic over and round the dunes, up and down, falling down in the sharp marram and the sand, running till I can't breathe any more and I don't know where I left him, so it's too late to change my mind. He'll just sit and sit and sit till something happens to change his mind. Only maybe nothing will and he'll just turn into a little

115

skeleton. I don't want to think that thought so I push it away. He'll be all right. Some wet tourist will find him and cart him off to a better life with someone who actually wanted a dog in the first place.

Don't look back don't think don't remember don't make a picture in your head or it will never go away just stomp into the wind and back to Nan's for tea where Mum and Nan sit in stony silence over the scones, Nan with her bruised face and Mum with her loose drunk's mouth and no one mentions Dad. They ask where the dog is, though. I say I lost him. Two hours of interrogation later and I can see Nanbread doesn't believe me but I stick to my story so there's nothing she can say. Mum doesn't even ask, just has a slug of whisky and heads off out. I ask Nan if Mum's found a man or something but I just get an earful about my generation think of nothing else but sex and no it isn't a man it's worse than that but she won't say any more.

There's this one place. When I was about five I remember this thing on telly called *The Secret Garden*, all about this boy in a wheelchair and a girl and they find this garden and it's behind a wall, you go through a gate and there you are. There was a gardener's boy in it called Dickon, and me and Susan Taylor used to get the giggles about his name because we knew Dick was a rude word. Well, we were only young. Anyway, on the island there's a garden and it's got a high wall and a gate and it's open to the public sometimes but most of the time it's locked.

It's near the castle, just sitting in the middle of a field full of sheep. Grey gate. Funny wall, three sides are tall and the one nearest the castle is low and I can climb up there and jump down inside, no problem, so I do this. There's flowers in there and a few veg, and a brick path and a bench and a sundial. I can sit on the bench and look at the castle and imagine that it's mine and this is my secret garden and no one can touch me while I'm in here. Only one day I'm lying flat out on the bench staring up at a big seagull floating above me, wondering if it's going to shit on me and suddenly there's the noise of someone unlocking the gate and I sit up and there's this man. He tells me to get out.

"Are you the gardener?" I ask him. He doesn't answer, just goes to a shed in the corner and starts to unlock it. I suppose that's my answer.

I don't want to stay anyway if he's here. It's all spoilt now. I head for the gate, kicking a few tall pink flowers on my way. He doesn't turn round. I snap the head off a purple one and crumble the petals on the path. He sees this all right. But doesn't say anything.

I ask Nan about him. She says he's American and his name is Jack. I don't fancy him or anything, but he's the only person on this island who isn't interested in me and what I get up to, so I start to wander over to the castle every day and if this Jack's in the garden I sit in the shadow of the wall on the outside and watch him through a chink. It's sort of peaceful. He knows I'm watching him, but he never for a second looks at me or says anything or comes my way, but I know he knows. Don't ask me how. He spends hours doing very small things. Kneeling on the stones with his hands in the flowers pulling out tiny weeds. Moving things from small pots to bigger ones. Digging things up. Mixing up stuff in buckets and then slopping it over the plants. And never a word. And no radio. When tourists come and squeal and potter about and swoon over the roses, he just looks at them and doesn't smile. Answers their questions and then goes back to doing whatever he's doing. He sounds like a film star. Deep brown voice, talks slowly, like he's thinking very hard before he speaks. Brown hair going grey round the edges. Brown skin from days and days and days spent out here in the sunshiny wind of a Holy Island summer.

One day I'm up there squatting in my usual place, sun on my back, tiny line of tourists heading up the hill out of the corner of my eye telling me the causeway's open and suddenly this whirlwind leaps at me from nowhere and jumps all over me, quivering and desperate. It's the fucking dog. How the hell did it get here? It's at least a week since I left him on the North Shore sitting obediently in that cave waiting for me to say the okay that would never come. I wish I'd killed it, but I wouldn't know how, I haven't got the guts to do it anyway. Furious, I push it away and shin over the garden wall. It yelps and tries to follow until I shove it back, and then it cowers by the gate, waiting for me. Jack is busy tying roses to wires and doesn't even turn round. I go over to where there's a ball of twine on the ground near him. I pick it up. He looks at me for the first time. Then he sticks his hand in the pocket of his jeans and pulls out one of those small red thingies with lots of knives and bottle openers and things for getting stones out of horses' hooves and all that. He opens a small blade, and hands it to me. I unravel some of the twine and cut, then I hand him back the knife. He turns away like it never happened. I attach the string to the dog's collar and drag it away across the damp green meadow towards the harbour. I can feel in my neck that Jack has stood up and is watching me as I march the dog away.

This time I drag it over the shingle until I'm round the side of the Herring Houses out of sight, by a row of lopsided tarred sheds, and I grab one of the old lobster pots dumped there and struggle with it up onto the Heigh, where some tourists are taking photos of the priory below and all smile at me because I look like I'm doing something quaint and seafaring and lobsterish with my faithful dog in tow. I drag the dog and the lobster pot down the shingly slope to the small beach where the lifeboat shed stands. Away round the back, the locals never come here, there's no lifeboat any more. I wedge the pot against the wall, shove the dog inside and struggle to pull down the lid. The dog sits peering at me hopefully from inside its prison. It's looking a bit thin. I walk away. It'll be all right. In the morning the birdwatchers up on the

Heigh will see it through their binoculars and before you know it he'll be crossing the causeway to a bowl of Pal Meaty Chunks and a better life all round. I can hear it yelping, so I go a bit faster until I can't hear it any more, only the sound of the waves crashing onto the rocks by the castle. There's going to be a storm. No one'll find him tonight, not while they're busy lashing things down and getting their boats in and worrying about sandbags being in the right place and all that. And Jack never speaks to anyone, so Nan won't find out. My heart is bumping. I tell myself as I scramble back up to the Heigh and see the castle looming out of the blackening sky that I won't turn and look back at the garden, but I do and I can't help it I'm disappointed because there's no Jack watching me.

"Your mother's seeing the vicar again," Nan says gloomily when I go home. She's sitting at the kitchen table shelling peas.

"Pardon?"

"That's the new man in her life. You were asking. I'm telling. No." That last because I've found mum's cigs on the sideboard.

I put them back. "Does she fancy him?"

Nan stares at me, with that bemused look on her face she gets whenever I say something she considers to be not on.

"Worse than that," she says. "I think it's the Lord she's after."

"Lord who?"

Nan sighs and shoves the folded newspaper full of fat peapods in my direction. Seeing as I can't have a cig, I might as well. I start pressing the taut pod ends, watching her to see how it's done, then squooshing the peas out into the colander with my finger. I'll never be as fast as her.

She doesn't answer. We sit in silence for a while, the only sound the rattle of peas hitting metal. Then she says, "Has she got sins need forgiving, your mam?"

I lower my head. "No. Don't think so."

"Only generally when people suddenly go all religious it's for a reason."

It's me, it's me, it's bound to be me.

I say nothing, feeling my ears going pink. She changes the subject. "Saw you coming from the Herring Houses just now. You been visiting that Yank?"

"No." I concentrate on the peas. What does she mean?

"Only if you don't live in the Herring Houses, which you don't, and you're not going out fishing with the Redpath lads, which I'm sure you're not, then there's only one reason to be over there, and that's to visit that Yank in his shack."

I'm silent. I eat a pea. So that's where he lives.

The front door crashes and Nan gets wearily to her feet as the Matching Red Anoraks (Room Two) are heard entering, windswept and exhilarated after a day on Hadrian's Wall. Nan goes out into the hall to make sociable noises and I hear them wittering on about how they only just made the causeway, water beginning to seep across the road, how exciting, storm brewing, sky like an oil painting, blah blah bloody blah.

A good moment to slip out, which I do. I'll do a bit of detective work. Over to the huts by the Herring Houses, taking Nan's poker from the kitchen range with me in case there's a padlock. There is – easy, and I'm inside. So this is Jack the Yank's kingdom, then. There's a room with a chair and a table covered with oilcloth, and a CD player and a mountain of books heaped up in stacks by the window. A pile of CDs all with this ugly miserable-looking bloke on the front called Jacques Brel, who must be French, judging from the titles of the songs, half of which I don't understand, which is peculiar, given my dad is French and I speak it without thinking. *Les Bigotes*. *Les Paumes du Petit Matin*. Too difficult for me. There's a gas ring and a sink in one corner. Beyond a curtain there's a bed. That's it. Not exactly smart. Could do with that ponce in the velvet jacket from *Changing Rooms* to come along and give it the once-over. There's a guitar propped against the wall by the books. I pick it up and twang it a bit but it's heavy, so I put it back. By the bed there's a heap of clothes, and a tin with an orange mountain on it. I open it, and it's like Christmas all of a sudden – a good ounce of nice dark crumbly stuff, and papers and some rolling tobacco. Heaven has come to Holy Island.

I'm busy smoking my way through a nice fat joint and

drinking a cup of tea made with one of his tea bags, feet up on the little table feeling like Goldilocks when the door suddenly opens and there he is, standing in the doorway. He's holding the poker I dropped by the door after I'd smashed the padlock. I don't move, deciding to be a brazen hussy, wait to see what he'll do, although I'm scared and he's frowning. It's a long moment.

Then he says he wouldn't mind a cup of tea himself and would I mind taking my feet off the table. I'm so surprised that he hasn't told me to piss off I get up and fill the small saucepan with water again and light the gas ring. He stands next to me, silent, washing his hands, like he has girls in his hut every day smoking his dope. Maybe he does.

"What's your name?" he asks finally. As if he didn't already know. He props up the bar of the Red Lion every night and I know I'm the hot gossip in there.

"Joanna." Silence. "And you're Jack."

"Yup."

He's picked the joint out of the ashtray where I'd hastily stubbed it out. He looks at it as if he's studying the workmanship. He won't find anything wrong with it. I may have been useless at school, but I could always roll a good spliff. He puts it back in the tin with the orange mountain on the front.

I don't know what's the matter with me. I feel nervous. I've finished mashing the tea bag around in the mug, and now I take it out and drop it in the sink. The milk's on

123

the drainingboard. I look at him. He nods. I pour the milk in.

"Sugar?"

He shakes his head.

I take the tea over to him, where he's sitting at the table. I sort of imagine he'll offer me his seat, as it's the one and only chair, but he doesn't. So I sit on the edge of the table, making sure I don't touch him at all, even though he's close.

"So," he finally says, looking at me for the first time. "What is it you want to know?"

"Nothing." I stare out of the grimy window, to where the beach is a blur of yellow darkened by the clouds overhead, pretending that everything else in the known universe is more interesting than him.

"So why are you here?"

Good question. I take a deep breath and then I give him the big interrogation – mainly to keep anything difficult from happening, because I'm scared, because I don't know why I'm here, because I like the sound of his voice. How old is he? Where's he from? What's he doing here? What was he before he came here? What's America like? To my amazement, he answers the questions slowly, one by one, seeming to give each of them a lot of thought as if he was on *University Challenge*. He's "fiftyish". He's from Chicago. He used to be a musician "way back" and now he's retired. Why here?

"To get a bit of peace." He looks at me to see what I'm

going to ask him next. It's incredible. I can feel this funny current fizzing between me and him, and for the first time since I arrived on this shithole of an island I can feel myself stirring. No. It's more than that: I think it's for the first time in my life. I think this must be lust. This must be what goes on when Gaby looks at me in that special way, when that prat Baz from the farm tries to get his hand up my skirt. It says in all the magazines that women – girls – we – I – can feel it too, but I never have, not till now. This is weird for me, a new thing. But I know what to do. I've had sex enough times to know you do the same things to all men, so here goes – the first move in an unimaginable idea – sex that I want. That thing called desire. So I reach across the table and touch him. And you wouldn't believe it, he pulls away. He's disgusted. He pushes his chair back. His face has changed. You're just a kid, for God's sake, he says. I can't believe it. I'm offering it to him on a plate, and he's saying no.

I want to weep from the humiliation, but instead I get up and tell him he's a dirty old man putting his hands on me and I'm going to tell. He says nothing. The angrier and louder I get the more still he is. Alice in Wonderland again. I seem to be shrinking and he seems to be growing. I leave, angry and loud and small, and shut the door. Damn. I've forgotten Nanbread's poker.

I'm hurrying across the shingle, rain beginning to wet my face, head down against the wind racing away from my humiliation and the dog appears again, like a maniac, pleased to see me, leaping at me, stinking of fish and whimpering. Why are dogs so stupid? I can't believe it's still here, still surviving, so determined to find me. Crazy with anger, I drag the dog across the field towards the castle, sobbing in the drenching bone-shattering rain that's teeming out of the sky and blinding me and wetting me through to my underwear, dog whining and slippery but coming with me – so stupid I could throttle it, and we stagger past the miserable sheep huddled in little damp gangs round the Bibly Hill, and we slide past the walled garden (don't look don't look you'll see his face and then you'll want to die some more) and on almost to the far wall, squelching through the boggy ground ankle-deep in mud and the rain still coming and the sky as black as night until we get to a crumbling old sheep-pen and I take the belt off my jeans and I loop it through the dog's collar then I buckle the belt to a rusty old metal ring in the pen. This is it. The pen is miles from anywhere. Now the dog can't find me, can't follow me, it can't sneak off and find food, it can't show up like a bad penny in times of trouble. I don't want to be loved, not by a dog, not by anyone. It will die and I will be left in peace. It whimpers as I stagger away into the storm.

I want to retreat. Back to the attic and the Scott Walker pictures and the songs and the dreams and the chink in my mother's armour, but there's no let-up. One night weeping in my bed with the record player turned up loud and the Walker Brothers belting out 'My Ship is

Coming In' and then it's morning and the storm has died and Mum decides we've got to go on a trip to some lighthouse in the middle of fucking nowhere. I say as much when I'm dragged out of my bed at the crack of dawn and made to eat breakfast in the kitchen and Nan points out that if you look beyond the castle you can see the Farnes and Longstone and didn't I know about Grace Darling, she rowed out and saved a load of blokes who were drowning in a ship, her and her dad. I said I wasn't interested. But I knew the light of the lighthouse. I could see it flashing green in the night from my window, regular, always, the light flashing on and off.

Billy's taking us in the school minibus, and he's outside hooting so Nan steps out with us to wave us off and there on the doorstep is her poker. I can feel my neck going scarlet but Nan picks it up without a word, frowns, and then props it up against the step while we climb aboard the bus. Then it's off down the A1 to Seahouses, me and Mum and a few nosy islanders and Billy watching me like he does in the rear-view mirror but saying nothing. I know he hates me, I don't know why exactly.

And it's a hot bus-ride before we get to Seahouses and we're standing on the quayside and there's a sign saying Billy Shiel's Boat Trips Established 1918 and my mum is studying the trips on the board – "Tour One, Inner Farne – that one goes to the Lighthouse," she says, as if this is the best news she's had all week. "A landing will be made on Inner Farne," she reads out loud from her leaflet, in a voice big enough to shame me, "where Saint Cuthbert spent the final days of his life . . . " I wander away and leave her to choose between the riveting prospect of one island covered with seals and birds and a hut, or two islands covered with seals and birds and no hut, or even the five-hour-bring-a-packed-lunch ornithology special incorporating every possible hut, bird and seal known to man. I just want to weep. This is me escaping the island – and what do I find? Adverts for more islands and another village, only this one's not quite so interesting because it hasn't got a castle and a causeway and more rabbits than you could dream of and the silence of the island – it's just a village with sea and boats and lobster pots but no magic. I don't want to go to the poxy lighthouse.

I wait till Mum is about to pile in the boat with a lot of grinning old eager camera-carrying bastards in shiny macs, just at the point where some red-faced young fisherman is about to help her in, then I say "I'm not coming".

She teeters, hesitates. "Joanna . . . " she says. Everyone on the boat waits.

"I'll meet you when Billy comes back with the bus," I say.

"But I wanted you to see –"

I'm hurrying away. I know she won't want to cause a scene, not here, not when she's so keen to go. "I've got enough money for chips," I shout, heading for the shops. I don't stop till I reach the top of the hill above the little harbour, and there's the boat, bobbing away on enormous waves, rolling its way out to the Farnes, Mum a sad blob in a red sunhat, waving at me. I pretend I haven't seen, and go to the nearest arcade.

I've fiddled a quid on some machine and the man has chucked me out but I've still got the money so I decide I'll go in a snack bar and have chips, get out of the wind, and I've got my chips in a plastic container with a little wooden fork and I'm going to a table when suddenly there's Jack, sitting by the window, drinking a mug of tea, not doing anything much, just sitting. I stand there not knowing what to do. It's a small place. Four tables. One's got a snuffly girl snogging her pimply boyfriend, and there's two other empty ones and there's Jack's. What am I supposed to do? We live on the same island. This is stupid. I go and sit opposite him. I don't look, though. I eat my chips. Silence. I sneak a peek. His eyes flicker towards me. "Hi," he says.

We sit there. We don't say anything. I offer him a chip and he takes one. I don't say I'm sorry to Jack and he doesn't say he's sorry to me. But I know it's all right again. I could weep.

I watch his brown fingers making a roll-up. The tin with the picture of the orange mountain on it is on the table. He catches me looking at it.

"Uluru," he says. I pick it up and look closer. "The Australians call it Ayers Rock."

"It's in Australia?" He nods. "You've been there?"

129

"For a while." He stares out of the window again, his eyes looking somewhere into the far distance, as if Australia is out there, which I suppose it is.

I think about him wandering the world – Australia, England, such a long way from America, from his home. And I'm singing a little Scott Walker song in my head, because I'm happy. *My ship is coming in* . . . And I'm hearing Scott Walker's dark, warm voice and looking at those brown hands opposite me on the table, and I give a little gasp, and Jack looks at me suddenly and looks away again – because he's guessed that I've guessed.

You see, I know who he is. It changes everything. Every single thing. I know who Jack really is. I know!

Chapter Six

O the bonny fisher lad that brings fishes frae the sea
O the bonny fisher lad gat haud o'me
On Bamboroughshire's rocky shore
Just as you enter Boomer Raw
There lives the bonny fisher lad,
The fisher lad that bangs them a'.

from SONGS OF NORTHERN ENGLAND

Martha Redpath got married today, to Jamie Lang's big brother Jason. Martha stopped me last week and said I could bring my family to the church if I wanted, and to the reception. My family! I never think of them like that. Half of me thought maybe I'd say nothing, go on my own, but that skinny girl needed a bit of entertainment, and Cath – well, anything to keep her sober for a few hours.

Martha was truly bonny, in a white rustling gown that

billowed out in the wind and a long veil that threatened to float away altogether and get tangled in the laurels round the churchyard. And Jason, who was never a handsome lad, ramrod-backed in his kilt, a fearful look in his eye, hair in a ponytail – "Thinks he's Mel Gibson," my daughter remarked dryly from her observation post by the Charlton grave. I said nothing. It's what I hated most about her being in my house, in my village, on my island – that cynicism about everything. She couldn't enjoy herself. She never let go. Always standing a little apart, watching, amused, while the rest of us got stuck in. And as for Joanna, she was staring at Martha and Jason and chewing her nails, her face unfathomable as the island lads lined up with their twelve bores and let off a ragged volley of shots up into the blustery sky to our cheers. As they ran off to tie the church gates and Martha and Jason stood with the Redpaths and the Langs for photos, I saw Cathy take a sneaky swig from a bottle she was hiding in her handbag. Joanna was looking at me but then she looked away again, her face shrewish and inscrutable, as usual. I saw her suddenly straighten up and pull at her unruly hair. I followed her gaze. She had seen Jack the Yank standing over by the gate. He had not seen her.

"It's a custom," I said, going to stand next to her. She looked at me, shocked. She had been somewhere else entirely.

"What?"

"The word is 'pardon'. It's a custom. The lads tie the

gates, and then the bride and groom have to pay a toll,
like. For refreshments."

Jason and Martha were heading round the back of the
churchyard, with everyone following. I took Joanna's
arm, feeling her resistance, aware that Jack hadn't moved
yet. She was too interested in that fella by half.

"Come on," I said. "Cath!" – my best imperious tone –
and they came too, my daughter and my granddaughter,
round the corner with me to where Martha was giggling
and blushing and clutching on to Micky Reid and Ted
Armstrong, ready for jumping the petting-stone. She
gathered up the soft gauze of her veil and wound it round
her shoulders to keep it out of the way, and then lifted up
her skirts, revealing net petticoats and a glimpse of scarlet
suspender on a white-stockinged leg. The village lads
whistled and stamped, the two old men spat on their
hands and grinned, grabbed Martha by the elbows and
then they were off and running, and with a great scream
she leapt over the stone and landed perfectly, knees
slightly bent, white satin-clad feet neatly together, amid
the cheers of all of us.

"High-jump champion at school," I heard Martha's
mam explain to the vicar.

Cath seemed to be enthralled by the spectacle, in her
disgusted, snooty, city kind of way. "Like something out
of a medieval passion play," she said, "Or Jennifer Jones
in *Gone to Earth*."

Joanna suddenly spoke, making me jump. She often

does that. Just when you think she's gone to some private and invisible place inside her head and has locked you out, she speaks and knocks you sideways. "The men holding her have to be two of the island's oldest inhabitants," she told her mother. "And the bride mustn't stumble, or it's bad luck. If she jumps it all right, it means good fortune and fertility."

I looked at her. I wonder who told her that, as if I didn't know. Jack was standing behind us somewhere, arms folded, watching the shenanigans in the churchyard in that cool, quiet way of his. Martha and Jason were handing over fivers to the lads with their guns now, which meant the gates could be untied and the wedding party could troop off round to the Red Lion for the reception. Off they went, following a piper. Martha's mam told me they'd hired a band from Berwick for the do, but this was one of Jamie's uncles from Belford, looking grand in his kilt and making a beautiful sound.

"Maybe I shouldn't come . . . " Cath murmured. She liked to drink alone.

Joanna turned on her, sudden and savage. "You've *got* to come," she said between clenched teeth. Sometimes that girl behaved like she belonged in an asylum.

"Vicar'll be upset if you don't," I goaded Cath, who glared at me, but followed. Joanna said nothing, walking next to me as meek as a bird, her eyes on her feet. Jack was ahead, walking with one of the other castle wardens, and I knew Joanna had seen him.

I wish I understood what was going on, apart from the obvious. Joanna was spending a lot of time hanging about with that Yank. I had seen her only this morning, climbing the hill to the castle and him at the top, waiting for her, and then both of them away over to the garden together. And down by the Straight Lonnen I'd seen those work-experience boys from the Donald farm straighten up from their fence-mending and watch their progress, squinting in the cold sun, frowning and fidgeting in the dust.

I was wearing my blue floral two-piece in the hope that Billy would be in the bar of the Red Lion, casually having a pint and on the look-out for me; and there he was, in the corner by the photographs of the lifeboat, eyes crinkling at the corners and a quick nod in my direction, and I knew he'd be in the back room later for a dance. My spirits lifted.

Cath had got me a gin and tonic and Joanna a much-complained-about lemonade, and we settled on the hard-backed chairs round the edge of the room to watch the band warming up, young children skating across the polished floor in party frocks, old men in their suits looking like they wished they were out catching lobster, the women from the WI gathered together like a flock of overweight starlings, chitterchattering and overcrowding. Joanna sat next to me, banging an impatient foot against the chair leg and looking for Jack, who hadn't come through from the bar yet.

Billy had told me about Joanna and the library. He

stopped me outside the village hall, after the Verbena Hotel meeting. The meeting's once a fortnight now, just to keep an eye on that evil little toad Dennis Bannion, who shows up and waffles on about maintaining the integrity of the island and how tourism has moved into the twenty-first century and so must we. I'm on the anti-Verbena committee, with Jessie from the post office and Ted Armstrong. Sometimes no one comes to the meetings – just us three and the Bannion man. But they'll be sorry. One big Verbena Hotel and that'll be the end of the island. They'll be wanting a bridge after that. And look what happened to the Isle of Skye. Me and Jessie and Ted, we'll fight it to the death, that's our vow. I never thought the day would come when I'd agree with Jessie Bell over anything, but there. Misery acquaints a man with strange bedfellows, as Tommy used to say. I think Shakespeare said it before him, if I'm not mistaken, but Tommy was never a one for acknowledging his sources. Many was the time I'd hear him sounding off like Nye Bevan in the pub, and I'd be the only one to realise it was because he was pinching Nye's words straight out of the *Tribune*.

Where was I? With Billy outside the village hall, if I'm not mistaken. He told me Joanna had been to Berwick again, on his bus. I was surprised. Since she'd been hanging around with the Yank, she'd shown no interest at all in going off the island. Billy followed her. She went to the library. The library! And she came out with a book, which she had read intently all the way home on the bus. I wondered if she had suddenly gone mad, or if the Yank was actually teaching her something other than the obvious.

I waited to see what would happen, if she'd take the book with her on one of her visits to Jack's hut. But no. She left every day all right, but there was never any book. I was dying to know what she was reading, but I knew better than to ask. Never ask a teenager anything. On this particular day Joanna was gone away over to the Lough – I sent her there to look for the dog. I thought it could be lost in the dunes, although I doubted it. It was probably dead. Joanna didn't seem to be upset, but I wondered if she was guilty about kicking it all those times. The way it adored her, gazing up at her with those faithful eyes, trying to press its head in her lap under the dinner table until she shoved it away. I miss that dog.

Cath was watching *Home and Away* on the telly, starting on the whisky and murmuring to herself about soap operas and narrative strands or some such, so I knew I had plenty of time. Away I went up to the attic, to Madam's lair, with its Walker Brothers pictures and its heaps of dirty clothes and its smell of eau de toilette, on the hunt for the mystery library book. When I found it, on the floor under the bed, along with two cold cups of coffee and a stripy sock, it was a bit of a disappointment, really. A fat blue book, called *Scott Walker: A Deep Shade Of Blue*. I should have guessed. So much for my fleeting fancies of Joanna discovering history or literature or even socialism. Talk about recurring nightmare. Scott ruddy Walker.

I rooted about a bit more in the room, hoping to find some insight into this creature who lived under my roof. All right, I shouldn't have, I know. I have no excuse. Just nosiness. I'm an old woman. We lead quiet lives. It makes us nosy. I found this cryptic scribbled list, in Joanna's round, childish handwriting. I didn't understand it. It was divided into two columns, headed "J" and "SW". Under the "J" column were scribbled the words "Jacques Brel, Bourbon, Paris, Ingmar Bergman, Existentialism." The same words were written in the second column, under "SW", and in addition the word "Jacky". I did really begin to wonder then if Joanna had gone mad.

I stared at the book for a moment, turning it in my hand. There he was on the cover, eyes hidden by dark glasses, unsmiling as usual. I opened it and read a bit of the blurb on the sleeve. *Life of seclusion . . . lonely childhood in Hamilton, Ohio . . . the truth about his years of fame . . . his singing partners and lovers . . . why he disappeared from public view . . .* Why did this man draw my daughter and in turn her daughter into some strange hypnotic world where he was the only thing that mattered? I put the book back where I found it. I had been a silly girl once myself. Had a terrible craze for a young lad who worked at the Hall stables. The sight of him exercising a horse through the woods was enough to turn my knees to jelly. But nothing like this. He died out in Greece somewhere, during the war. Would I have felt the same if he had only disappeared? Would I still be harking on about him, years after those first girlish yearnings? I didn't know. Because after he'd gone, there had been Tommy, and all the children. I had forgotten that lad almost completely. Funny, I couldn't even remember his name, just those dark eyes and a pair of strong brown hands against the foam-flecked sweating neck of a horse.

"Can I have some crisps, Nan?" It was Joanna, staring at me, dragging me back to the present. The band had started to play a medley of Beatles songs, and the room was filling up. All the islanders were coming to the reception, and there was already an atmosphere of rising excitement. I felt as though I'd been asleep. But of course I hadn't. I'd been wandering in the woods near Seahouses, wearing a pink organza Sunday-best dress, on the lookout for a string of racehorses and a boy with dark eyes.

I wanted to ask Joanna about Scott Walker, but I didn't. I asked her where her mother was.

"Where do you think?" Her face closed off again for a moment. "At the bar, buying herself a triple Scotch."

Joanna watched a couple of the village kids racing each other from the band to the emergency exit doors. "I've had an idea," she said, her face not visible to me.

"Really?" I said dryly, "And will it cost me money, this idea?"

I immediately regretted my tone, because Joanna suddenly turned to me, and for the first time she had what I can only call a real face – urgent, alive, anxious. It was a shock. I was used to her desiccated, withdrawn little face contorting into various expressions of mood, but I had never believed any of them. My eyes connected with hers.

"Come on, then, lass. Tell me," I said.

She sipped at her lemonade. "I've decided you and me should play Cupid," she said.

That was the last thing I expected to hear. I leaned towards her, interested. "Oh, aye? Who to?"

Her answer almost made me spill a good gin into the lap of my two-piece. "Jack the Yank," she said, "and my mum."

I tried to absorb this. "You want your mam to get together with Jack Dalton?"

"Is that his name? Yes." She started talking then, in hurried staccato bursts, like a scattergun. "He's the kind of man she should have married. You don't like my dad. Neither does she. And I know Jack. He's funny. And kind. He's a musician. He likes politics. They'd be perfect . . . " Her voice faded away. Jack had come into the room and was standing with the Redpath lad, chatting, drinking beer.

To say I was suspicious would be an understatement. This from the girl who spent all her time trying to get into men's underpants. In fact I had convinced myself that she had succeeded in penetrating the Yank's Y-fronts herself in recent weeks. Perhaps I had got it all hopelessly, horribly wrong. Perhaps I had imagined her to be more sophisticated than she really was. After all, as I had to constantly remind myself, she was only fourteen. This plan was straight out of *Bunty* magazine.

I looked at Jack. He was watching the dancers, listening to something Davy Redpath was saying. He looked smarter than usual, and I realised it was the first time I'd seen him in a proper jacket, although he was still wearing jeans. Not that anyone in the village would care – they were used to him by now. If he was aware that two pairs of eyes were studying him intently he didn't show it. I looked at his hand round the pint mug. Brown. Reminded me of someone. He'd got a strong jaw. Not a man to play about with. I must have been going soft in the head, but the gin was making me remember that Frenchman, and his black curls and foreignness, and my mistrust of him, and Cath's wreck of a life, and so I said yes to Joanna, I said yes I'd help her, I said yes I thought her mam and that Yank – why not? And suddenly Joanna came alive, and her eyes burned gratefully at me and we were a pair with a plan.

Things were warming up. Martha and Jason had arrived and were smooching in the centre of the floor, which was full of dancers of varying age and ability waltzing, or trying to, on the old polished floor. She went to fetch her mam from the bar. I took a deep breath and went over to where Jack was standing, alone now, propping up the doorpost and watching the band, who had lurched into a string of unrecognisable ballads.

"You not dancing?" I asked, unaccountably nervous, a smile glued to my face.

Not unsurprisingly, the Yank was a little taken aback at this sudden friendly overture from someone who hardly ever gave him the time of day. He gave me a quick look and then returned his gaze to the dancing.

"I'm not really the dancing type," he said.

"Joanna tells me you're a musician."

"That's right." I felt him glance down at me, slightly puzzled.

"Guitar, she says."

He didn't answer. An old chap from the village had got up on stage, as he did at every function, and had started playing his accordion. We watched the guests dancing and stamping in time to the music. There didn't seem to be a lot else to say. Fortunately Cath appeared, carrying a fresh drink for me and a large one of her own.

"Here," she said, handing me the drink, "Joanna said you wanted another one."

I took it from her, relieved. "I'll leave you to it," I said brightly, and scuttled away back to the chairs, where Joanna was watching, her face serious.

"Plan A in action," I said. We watched them surreptitiously. They stood together awkwardly, two strangers with nothing to say to each other. The music changed to a waltz.

"Ask her," I heard Joanna say grimly, under her breath, her tone savage. *"Ask her to dance!"*

But he didn't. For what seemed like an age they stood, occasionally exchanging a platitude or two or a polite, embarrassed smile. Joanna groaned. One of the work-experience boys, the taller, dark one, was suddenly standing in front of her. He didn't say anything, just looked at her insolently.

"Fuck off," Joanna said succinctly. I cringed, hoping the WI flock hadn't heard. He stalked off, seemingly unabashed. I don't understand the young. Joanna crashed down her glass of lemonade and went to the centre of the dance-floor where she proceeded to perform some strange snake-like dance completely alone, seemingly oblivious of the stares of the wedding guests. I sighed to myself. This was proving to be a disaster.

I glanced over to where Jack was trying to be polite to my drunk daughter. He was watching Joanna. I realised then. Whatever Joanna was trying to do to him, however much she wanted to make things right with her mam and to put this man in her path, she was wasting her time, because it wasn't Cath that Jack Dalton wanted: it was Joanna.

I felt cold. This was a bad day.

Billy came and asked me to dance and I allowed him to pull me onto the floor for the 'Gay Gordons'. I knew there'd be talk tomorrow, but I didn't care; I wanted to feel his reassuring arm on my shoulder, see his cheeky grin and feel like a girl again. I wanted the chill to go away.

"Saw that girl of yours the morn," he said, as we did a spirited turn.

"Cath?" I laughed, breathless. "Where were you? The bottom of a bottle?"

"Not her. Joanna. She was with that Yank, up in the castle garden. Drinking his tea, in the toolshed."

I felt the gladness draining away.

"Not saying anything, mind," he continued, forced to shout over old Walter Sharp's accordion. "Not saying anything. Just sitting."

"It's a gallop now, you old fool," I shouted, pulling him into line. I didn't want to think about Joanna with Jack Dalton, their peculiar intimacy. I wanted it to be like before. Me and Billy, dancing together, not a care in the world. Before they came.

Gradually the edge of the day softened into the blur of a September evening and I had a few gins too many and the brittle silhouette of my daughter faded away somewhere and I don't know what happened to Joanna; so when Billy persuaded me to go outside, all fired up by the band playing 'String of Pearls' and wanting a kiss, I went with him, and one thing led to another and before you could say Jack Robinson I was in the bus shelter with him, giggling like a schoolgirl and glad the dark had descended so no passing nosy parker could see.

Billy wanted me to invite him back to the house, a bit of malarkey with everyone out is what he said; but we wouldn't have been alone. A couple of Japanese pilgrims were staying in the front bedroom, and they'd be in the lounge now, watching *Casualty*, so I had to turn him down, rather regretfully I admit, what with the warm breeze and the gin and the excitement of the occasion.

We headed back to the Red Lion arm-in-arm, comfortable with each other, him sulking a bit but with a good heart. I was heading for the side door which led to the room where the band was playing, when he pulled me over to the front window.

"Your family fraternising with the enemy," he said.

I looked through the grimy glass into the smoke-filled bar. At first I couldn't see what he meant, only Joanna sitting at the bar eating crisps on her own, staring at her feet. Then next to her, I saw them. The rat, Bannion, all dressed up in his striped suit, and leaning all over him, laughing – *laughing!* – my daughter, Cath. He had a possessive hand on her arm and she was leaning towards him as he spoke, her eyes half-closed, her mouth curved upwards in a drunken smile.

I must have given a little yelp, because Billy was trying to hold me back, but I pushed him off and stalked inside, elbowing through the crowd at the bar waiting for drinks until I was there, in front of them, deafened by the noise from the band and half-blinded by the smoke.

I can't explain what happened. Perhaps it was just that

for the first time ever I suddenly saw myself as the mother of this woman, thirty years too late maybe, but then I wasn't in a fit state to weigh up the whys and wherefores. I pulled Bannion off his stool.

"Leave my daughter alone," I said. Conversation in the vicinity began to falter.

He brushed at his sleeve where I had touched him, as though I had dirt on my hands. "I'm buying your daughter a drink, Mrs Weatherson, that's all –"

Cath was staring at me, surprised, wobbling on her bar stool. "Mam . . . "

Funny. No child of mine had called me that publicly in a long time. I heard my voice coming out of me cold and hard, like it used to be when one of the bairns came in late and I was going to give them a dose of the belt hanging on the back of the pantry door. "Get yourself home, Catherine Weatherson."

She giggled a little, too drunk to comprehend. Bannion gave an angry snort, like a small pony. "I really don't think it's any of your business who she –"

Well, I saw red then. Literally. I hardly knew I was doing it, but I picked up Cath's drink from where she had left it on the bar and I threw it down the front of Bannion's white poplin shirt, and people cheered and whooped around me as though I'd hit the jackpot at housey-housey. And I said it again, only louder this time, egged on by Billy's grinning face and the laughter, "Cath. I said home."

And lo and behold, she went, sidling out of the bar, lips wobbling, for all the world like she was twelve again and I'd caught her at the cake tin. Jimmy leaned across the bar towards me, ignoring Bannion and his dripping shirt. "Drink on the house, Sylvie," he said to me, grinning. "Best thing I've seen since Newcastle won the Cup."

I was about to decline, thinking I should follow Cath home and make sure she didn't do anything stupid, when suddenly there was a kerfuffle nearby, and I turned to see Joanna wrestling with that boy from the farm, the work-experience lad, the one who had asked her to dance. I say wrestling, but it was a bit one-sided, Joanna with her arm round the boy's throat, his face going puce. Then he managed to get a grip on her hair and yanked her head backwards, choking and cursing, as his two friends joined in, grabbing at Joanna, calling her names, spitting out ugly words as the wedding guests backed away. Before I could move there was someone else there, lunging at the lads, hauling the smallest one off and throwing him against the bar as if he were an insect to be swatted away. I stood frozen as Jack Dalton prised the tallest boy off Joanna and struggled to keep the third one at bay. Then as fast as it had happened, it was over. A couple of village men had pulled Jack off and Billy and Jimmy were hauling the work-experience boys out of the door. The band was still playing 'Delilah'. Jack straightened up and walked away towards the music. Joanna wiped blood from her lip.

"Come on, bonny lass," I said. "Time to go."

And we left the pub.

We walked home in silence, apart from me telling her she was what boys call a tease, and that she should start using what she had above her waist, for a change. She didn't answer.

When we got in, the Japanese pilgrims had gone to bed, and Cath was watching *Newsnight* and weeping into yet another glass of whisky. I was too shaken to sleep, so I sat and watched the telly with her as Joanna thumped off upstairs to bed. Trouble in Bosnia, a rugby match, an interview with a politician. It was on, but not in my head, if you know what I mean.

I must have nodded off. The next thing I knew there was someone knocking on the front door and the tv was murmuring and Cath slumped on the sofa, mouth agape, sleeping.

It was Micky Reid. I remembered how they had knocked in the past, when there was a storm and the boats were out, or if the lifeboat had been called, but not this time.

"Fire," he said briefly, before hurrying on. "Down by the harbour. Looks like the Herring Houses."

Joanna had been on the stairs, listening. As I pulled my coat on, she clattered down, leather jacket over her nightie.

"You need shoes," I pointed out.

She pulled on some wellingtons and followed me out. Cath hadn't stirred.

We could see the blaze almost as soon as we stepped out of the door. Joanna started to run. I stood breathless on the step for a moment, looking at the flames snaking up into the dark sky. Down by the harbour I could see the dark figures of village lads racing about with hoses. The causeway was under ten feet of North Sea, so there was going to be no fire engine. It was a wedding night Martha and Jason would remember forever.

By the time I reached the Herring Houses the flames had subsided, and there wasn't a lot to see, only the charred and smoking crossbeams from the roof, collapsing in spitting heaps on the sand, and the smell of burned lino. Jack Dalton was standing with some of the men surveying the ruins of what had once been his home, his face blackened from the smoke, his eyes red-rimmed and tired. Jessie Bell was standing next to me, a coat on over her dressing-gown.

"Someone saw some lads running away," she said. "Whoever would want to do a thing like this to Jack Dalton?"

I said nothing, watching Joanna pick her way through the warm embers of what had once been Jack's front door until she was standing with him, a defiant gesture of friendship. They exchanged a few words, and suddenly he looked up and fixed his gaze on me, frowning a little, one grimy hand smearing a streak across his forehead. Joanna approached.

"I told Jack we'd put him up," she said bluntly. I could feel Jessie's eyes turning to her, curious. "Is that all right?"

What could I say? Particularly as it felt as if the fire was Joanna's fault. And I wouldn't see anyone homeless. I nodded, and she went to fetch him. The crowd had begun to drift away, people patting Jack on the back and murmuring apologetically.

He came across. "Is it okay?"

"Of course, lad. Come away home." Joanna was looking at me, something akin to gratitude on her face.

When we got back and found Cath bleary-eyed in front of a late tv film, I remembered then – the pact, the matchmaking. No wonder Joanna wanted him to stay. She hurried off to bed. I stood in the doorway of the living-room.

"Room number four at the back," I said to him. "I'll go and unlock it and get you a towel –"

Cath was staring up at him from the sofa, a little disorientated by his blackened face. She held up a bottle. "Drink?"

He looked at me, struggling between politeness and trauma. I felt sorry for him, all of a sudden.

"Go on, then," I said. "If ever a man needed a drink –"

He sat down on the edge of my armchair. I tried not to wince, thinking about what state the cushions would be in tomorrow. I left them to it. *Che sarà sarà*, to quote

Doris Day. Perhaps Joanna's dream would come true after all.

Me, I slept a strange, blank, dreamless sleep, punctuated only by the sound of a dog, whimpering somewhere in the dark.

Chapter Seven

I think we were probably the drunkest group ever.

Scott Walker, 1973
(from SCOTT WALKER: A DEEP SHADE OF BLUE)

Gaby, I miss you. In the living-room on my own. Me and my bottle. Catherine Mary Lefèvre, née Weatherson and Johnny Walker, my amber friend. The television's on, and my eyes have swivelled towards the screen, but there's a blurred film of soft tears between me and the smirking weatherman's prediction about tomorrow. It doesn't matter, because I know. Don't have to look at the thundercloud sitting on his map right on top of the island to know that tomorrow it will rain. And the wind will blow and bite and I won't feel like going out again, except to see David, the vicar, who talks to me in a dark brown voice about God and gives me sweet sticky tea in the inviting dark of the vestry when everyone else has gone away. The church is like a cradle, I feel enveloped in its calm and for a while the bad thoughts about my life trickle away and I'm loved by someone. God.

My mother is a total bitch. She's a cold, granite-faced harpy with no love in her heart for me, or my brothers and sisters. Is it any wonder we have all gone as far away from her as we can? Jess and John in Australia, Mary in London, Susan in Ireland, just Tom and David in Newcastle, and they only visit her at Christmas, because they feel guilty and dutiful. They don't love her, any more than I do. Why should we love her? The only tears she ever shed was for the one of us that died, baby Alice, whom we none of us remember at all. Weeping for a dead child and dry eyes for the living, that's my mam. She should be weeping for me. I came back here because I was hurt and when you are hurt you go to your mother, you trust your mother to hold you and comfort you and make the hurt go away. Only not my mother. Not Sylvie Weatherson. That film – *Mommie Dearest* – the one where Faye Dunaway's being Joan Crawford and beats her kids with a clothes-hanger? She had nothing on our mam.

Joan Crawford. *Mildred Pearce*. Wonderful film. The suffering of mothers. And how we suffer.

Someone came to the door just now and woke me up. Joanna was out there, I heard her voice. She and Mam left, slamming the door. Then there were voices shouting in the street, someone running. I remember the wedding, and being in the bar and a man called Dennis buying me a drink; not a nice man particularly, but he reminded me of London and the world I come from, not this rough and lonely place where I should feel as though I belong but I don't. Katy Brown arriving on the Deadwood stage in *Calamity Jane*. That's what I feel like. Everyone else in buckskins and I'm in velvet. Only she had her life ahead of her, and mine is over.

Gaby, *mon mari*, I miss you.

The front door is unlocked. Joanna is suddenly in the doorway staring at me, her cheeks enflamed, a peculiar look in those birdy eyes. Then she's gone and instead there's Mam in her coat and a tall man standing looking down at me with a burned face. Mam speaks to him and he answers only I can't follow. Sounds like they're underwater. Then she goes and he's sitting in her armchair and I understand then that I've offered him a drink.

"Is there a glass?" he asks. He's an American. I realise his face is not burned, only covered in dirty streaks. Is he a gypsy? Mam would never let a tinker in here. And anyway, do Americans have gypsies? Are there American gypsies?

He's gone away to the kitchen. I hear water running in the sink. I turn back to the film. I hope he's brought his own bottle. Tyrone Power is being a stablehand, and George Sanders has just whipped him with a riding-crop.

155

Not a good idea. I get up and change channels, almost falling into the fireplace on the way back. Mam wouldn't have a remote control. Make life too easy, wouldn't it? It's pop music, some old black and white film. The Troggs singing 'I Can't Help Myself'. The man has come back. He's washed his face and I realise I not only know him, but I've already met him once today, at the wedding. He picks up the whisky bottle and pours himself a great big measure and then knocks it back. Bloody cheek. He's back in the armchair. Looking at the telly. I look too.

"Troggs," I tell him. He doesn't say anything, just watches. "New industry, nostalgia. Didn't have it in my day. Didn't all long for the return of Fred Astaire," I say. Well, we didn't, did we? We were of the moment. We thought our music was best, our clothes were best, our drugs. Not like kids now. They just want what we had, only they never get it quite right. Manic Street Preachers. Body-piercing. Ecstasy. Doesn't quite cut the mustard.

I watch him pouring himself another drink. He's nearly cleaned me out, the bastard. He seems to be lost inside his head somewhere, just drinking and staring at the screen. The Troggs turns into the Lovin' Spoonful.

"Nineteen sixty-six," he says suddenly. "Kama Sutra label."

"How very male of you," I observe into the bottom of my glass.

We maintain a companionable silence. "Did you ever see them?" I ask him finally, "In America?"

156

"Nope. You?"

I think hard. Nineteen sixty-six, I was nineteen. "Too early for flower power . . . " I'm thinking aloud. Then I remember. "Mam said she bought me a ticket . . . "

"Sorry?"

"For my birthday. For a concert. She bought me a ticket. I was at university."

"You were?" He's sitting forward in the armchair, his legs stupidly too long for that small plump chintzy thing. "Which one?"

"London School of Economics. You?"

He shakes his head. "Didn't go."

The tv gets suddenly louder as a group of screaming monochrome mini-skirted girls race round a corner in pursuit of the Kinks. They'll all be menopausal now. The American leans over and pours me another drink. Then he drains the bottle into his own glass. We both drink.

"Politics," I hear a voice – my voice – saying. "My mother was into politics, so I had to go and live out her dream."

"You didn't like politics?"

I try hard to think of the answer to that one. I did all the stuff I was expected to do: the activism, the demonstrations, the sit-ins, the pamphlet-writing. But my heart just wasn't there. It was with Scott Walker. I take another drink. "Pot," I say. "I smoked a lot of pot."

"Me too," he says.

"Smoked a lot of pot, wore great clothes. Went to concerts."

"Uh-huh."

"Then I left. I never got my degree."

My failure seems to sit like a stone between us. The silence jangles, suddenly. Bo Jangles. I get up, and go into the kitchen. I've got another bottle hidden away behind the compost bucket under the sink, with Mam's pile of used carrier bags acting as a blanket.

When I return, he's leaning back, eyes shut. I wonder if he's asleep, but even as the thought wobbles into my head I realise he's looking at me. I pour myself another generous drink and another one for him. It's nice to have a bit of company.

"So you left the university." His hands are resting on the square floral arms of the sofa. The fingernails are black with grime. "Then what?"

"You're a nosy sod," I tell him, and laugh. I'm not normally rude, but you know what they say about *in vino veritas*. But the truth is I rather like him, I like the fact he's interested in me and who I am and what I've done. He's asked more questions in the last five minutes than my god-forsaken mother has asked me in thirty years. "I wandered about," I say, fingering my whisky glass and tracing the diamond shapes as they catch the light from the standard lamp. "Amsterdam. I spent some time in Holland." I don't tell him I was looking for a fucking pop star, do I? It seems the life of a sad sod now when I look at it.

"Great dope in Amsterdam," he says. "Particularly in the seventies."

Who is this guy – Howard Marks? "Then I came home." I'm not going to let him tell me about his European tour when I'm trying to tell my life story. He can wait. "I worked in a health food shop for a while." A while! Three years in that little cupboard with the smell of wheatgerm and Mr Andrews in his white coat pretending to be a scientist. Three whole years of weighing out pulses into paper cones.

"And then?"

"A bookshop. Not just your average bookshop. An alternative one. In Camden. You know. *International Times*. Oz. That kind of thing."

"*Prairie Fire*," he says, to himself. I don't know what he's talking about. Then he suddenly seems to pull himself together and I feel his focus return to me. "And where did you meet your husband?"

"Around that time, I suppose. I can't remember. I'm useless at dates. Only he was gay, it turned out." I hear a hard, harsh laugh. It's mine. "Probably I drove him to it."

"Joanna's father was gay?" His eyes have widened in surprise.

"Gaby? No . . . he was much later. Oh . . . much later." I've never been very good at dates. I'm thinking back to Paul, with his lanky legs encased in purple loons, his hunted look, his shame. Times were different then. I wonder if he's still alive. Probably not. He was always one of those people that things happen to. Like a wife, when you know you don't want one. I expect he went down in the first wave of the Aids epidemic, knowing him. I haven't wondered about him for years. And now his face swims before me, that anguished just-slapped look he always had that I despised so. *Cathy, I'm sorry.*

Gaby, I miss you.

"Gaby." The American has said this and it wakes me up. He says Gaby's name slowly.

"Gabriel. He's French."

"Ah." He's getting drunk. I've slowed down now, but then I had a serious headstart. But he's definitely knocking back a lot of booze.

"Changed my life. Lousy life. Lonely. Bedsits. Bad sex. Then he came along – Gaby. Half my age."

"He was?" The guy is listening intently. I'm enjoying myself. A captive audience. A willing audience. Someone listening. And he has a kind face. He was probably handsome once, in a butch kind of way. But not beautiful, like Gaby.

"Exotic. Black curls. Where Joanna's come from. Black. Not like me. Horrible ginger, ghastly Northern trait, borders hair, Geordie colouring . . . "

I tell him all about Gaby and he's very attentive, eyes watching mine, his body still, apart from when he gulps another slug of Johnny Walker. I tell him about Gaby's beauty, how exotic he seemed to me, smoking Gauloises, unshaven, opinionated. Also feckless and lacking in intellect, but I didn't discover these qualities until it was too late and we were married. I tell the Yank I think Gaby probably married me so that he could stay in England. Paris had become an impossible place, he said. He couldn't go back. I wonder now if there was some other reason: a crime committed, a child, perhaps, or an angry husband of some bourgeois housewife Gaby had seduced. He will never tell me. Would never tell me.

I tell Jack – that's his name, he informs me, as if I didn't know, what with Joanna hanging round him all day – I tell him about how my pregnancy came like a gift from heaven. Now I could keep this angelic boy as my lover, because my pregnancy excited him, enthralled and bewitched him. I remember that time so clearly, because I think it's the only time I have ever been truly happy. The birth was difficult, but not earth-shattering. And the baby was beautiful, like her father. I called her Joanna after a song by Scott Walker, but I never told Gaby that. He liked the name. He said it over and over, in that accent of his: *Joanna. Joanna.*

Jack is twisting the glass round in his hands, seeming suddenly anguished. Then he stands up. "How about a walk?" He says.

I'm in no fit state, but tonight feels like an adventure, and so I find myself in Mam's old mac and Joanna's wellingtons, stumbling along in the dark by the seashore, trying to keep up with the American, who is carrying on like a man possessed. The sea is invisible, but I can hear its primeval roar and the sucking sound of waves receding across the shingle. This place gives me the creeps. *Cul-de-Sac*. Roman Polanski. And now me and this American, his face lit spasmodically by the moon sailing out from behind the low clouds as we splash in the shallows of the harbour, me following him like a drunken spaniel.

We stop down by the Herring Houses, and I smell charred wood and acrid smoke mixed with the salty tang of crabs. The boats are out.

"Is there a fire?" I ask.

"There was. My house." Is he joking? "Stay there," he says, and disappears into the darkness. I sit down obediently on a grassy mound facing the sea, and fall immediately asleep, my back resting against a beached dinghy. I dream about Gaby, of course. I see him and Joanna in a tangle on the sofa, and the puppy jumping at me with little cries of joy, and then the door opens and Mam is there, frowning, holding my Political History coursebooks in a pile, carrying them like a tea tray, Hobsbawm on the bottom. "Would you like beans or peas with that?" she asks me crossly. Then I'm awake again, because Jack has sat down heavily next to me with something that sounded like a sob. He's doing something in the dark. The rasp of a match and the quick brightness of its flare tells me it's a cigarette. No, a joint. He hands it to me. I take it.

The first intake of smoke and it goes straight to my head.

"We don't have sex any more," I hear myself telling him, to my surprise. I've said it now. I might as well continue. "He doesn't find me attractive – no," – this as he looks about to make a polite noise – "no. Don't. I know my time's up. We have to step aside. Make way for the young." He was listening, saying nothing. "You know how old Leonardo DiCaprio was when he made his first film? Drew Barrimore? And all those film-school movie brats in Hollywood . . . " I've lost track of what I'm saying. Silence.

"Maybe the young don't want us to step aside," he says, and I pick up my train of thought again.

"No. You're wrong. This is their world now. Not mine. Not yours. But trouble is, see, Gaby – he's younger. He doesn't belong with me, but he's too old to be young . . ."

My voice trails away. He's looking at me in the dark. We sit in silence.

"I've had my adventures," I say dully. "The sixties. That was my adventure. Yours too, I bet. You have that look."

"Yup." He's very still, looking out to sea.

"Not good enough. Want more detail. I showed you mine now show me yours." Still he says nothing. "Come on!" I'm struggling against sleep. "Won't tell, promise. Too drunk anyway. Probably won't remember in the morning."

He shifts a little and takes another toke on the joint. His silence is beginning to irritate me.

"Come on, Mister Jack Enigma," I say. "The sixties. Your adventure. Cough it up."

"You really want to know?"

"I just said I did, didn't I?" My eyelids are drooping. I sit up a little, trying to look alert, to keep myself awake. Then I sit dazed, listening to him as he starts to talk.

"I guess with your political education you know about what was going on in the States then."

"When?"

"When you were at your university," he says, taking the joint from my fingers and inhaling on it deeply. He hands it back. I drift back to the cold support of the boat against my spine. He's not waiting for an answer. "I was in New York. The Village," he says, "Kenmore Avenue. Making bombs." I can hear the creaking of old chains in the sea, and the rustle of creatures in the grass. "You ever hear of the Weather Bureau?"

It's just as well he can't see me, because I can feel my jaw literally drop. "Of course I have," I manage to say, feeling suddenly cold and almost sober, abruptly aware of the damp grass against my thighs. "You were one of those people?" His silence is my answer and I burst out laughing, incredulous.

"I'm sitting on Holy Island with a real radical!"

He's talking, in a low voice, almost a drone, about himself. I can hardly take it in, although I hear the words. "You remember the Days of Rage in Chicago? We bombed a statue in Haymarket Square. It was the fall of sixty-nine. Then the SDS turned against us and after the National War Council we went underground . . . "

I remembered. They were always talking about it in the common room. A woman ran the organisation, they said. Sometimes people from the Weather Underground would come to London and shout at students in the Roundhouse, or we'd read about them, what they believed in – killing the pigs, trashing the establishment, wargasms, group sex, collectivism. They even praised Charlie Manson, I remember.

I can't see his face. A Weatherman sitting in the dark, sharing his joint with me. He's still talking. "Our goal was the destruction of US imperialism. We wanted a classless world. We thought we were guerillas."

Why is he telling me? Because I'm drunk and I've told him I'll forget? Because I went to LSE? Or because he can sniff out a weedy liberal at fifty paces?

"You don't need a Weatherman to know which way the wind blows," I say, grinning under cover of the black night. "Bob Dylan. *Blonde on Blonde*."

"How very male of you." His tone is dry. "Only it was on *Bringing It All Back Home*. First track."

"So what happened? Did you get caught? Were you in prison?"

"Nope." A long hiatus, broken only by the sound of a long, intense inhalation of smoke. "Some of my friends died. They made a bomb at their place in Greenwich Village and it went wrong and they blew themselves up.

The rest of us went into hiding. I moved to Paris. Gave it all up. Learned French. Worked in a bar. Became a model citizen."

"*Citoyen*," I said. I felt his hand on my arm, and just for a second I felt the warmth drain out of my blood. He had killed people. Now he had told me who he was.

But he was scrambling to his feet. "Come on," he said. "We may as well go back. There's nothing left here."

"Are you on the run?" I ask him as we trudge back together, almost companionable.

He thinks about that for a moment. "Not on the run," he says at last. "But running."

The last part of our journey home is carried out in silence. Perhaps he's regretting telling me these things. I don't want him to be sorry. Like John Travolta and Uma Thurman in *Pulp Fiction*, the atmosphere between us has been softened by our shared confessions. So when we get back, I offer him one for the road, a nightcap, and we're back in the living-room, one bar of the electric fire on even though it's August, and we're a long way down the second bottle. He seems to be miles away somewhere. Maybe he's making bombs. Me, I've got Gaby's face in front of me, his white-toothed smile, the disarming way he has of caressing one of his own curls, and his voice, saying *"We were just going to watch Seinfeld . . . "*

I start to weep. Not a decorous, Emma Thompson-style trickling tear from one corner of the eye, but horrible blubbing, a torrent streaming down my face and great shuddering sobs coming from somewhere deep inside me, more like Juliet Stevenson in *Truly, Madly, Deeply*. I can't stop. The American is silent, drinking.

"Do you know why I'm here?" I manage to ask him finally. He shakes his head. He's still not looking at me. "Because of Joanna," I say. Now he looks. Another one taken in by her moody prettiness, that perfect little body in its ugly clothes, that sulky, sultry fuck-off sexiness. "Interested now, are you?" I can hear my voice, shrewish, slurred. He doesn't reply, because he knows he doesn't have to. He knows I've got him sussed.

"Joanna Lefèvre," I say. "Fourteen going on thirty-five." It's like a stream that starts and can't stop, bouncing down the mountainside, hysterical bubbles and froth. "I found her groping my husband. Her father. My husband. Gaby. Together on the sofa, while I'm out trying to earn money —" I scrabble for one of Mam's tissues, plucking one from the box on the bookshelf, where it's balanced on a copy of *Inside the Left* by Fenner Brockway. "What they call a compromising situation. I know what you're thinking," this, as he opens his mouth to speak – "that it must have been him, that she's only a kid, doesn't know what she's doing. You're wrong. You're so wrong. She's not a kid. Never has been. She's been flirting with him since she was five. She's always seen me as the rival. Only how do you compete with a teenager, when you're getting older and your looks are going and you're worn out with working all the hours God sends —" He's staring at me, drink forgotten. Now the stream is gathering speed as it tumbles ever downwards. "I know you must think I'm not very maternal, that I should be defending her – but I can't – I know what she's like. I've watched her trying to seduce you in that garden of yours, playing prick-teaser to the local boys – she can't help herself, she's just a wayward little tart, any dick will do, the more forbidden the better. You ever see *The Omen*? Well, Damien wasn't a patch on her, believe me. She's devious as well, she knows how to divide people. That's why I'm here, Jack, because I believed the worst of my husband, I let her do that to me. Only I've decided. I'm going back. To London. I hate it here. I'm only here because of her and she doesn't need me. She doesn't need anybody. Did you know she killed our dog? A present from her father, and she kills it. Or at least she took it out and came back without it and gave us some cock-and-bull story we were supposed to swallow about it going missing. But I know her, I've had fifteen years of her, I know. She's a monster. She can do what she likes. She can go into care. She can stay here. I don't care."

I stand up, shakily. He's staring up at me. Finally he says into the silence, "How can you say she's a monster? She's just a screwed-up kid –"

I shouldn't have told him, I shouldn't have imagined for one minute that he'd understand. Of course not. He's enthralled by her, he's just like Gaby was. "No," I tell him, "no. She's not a kid. She's a young woman, a sexually aware young woman who knows exactly what she wants and how to get it. She's lying up there now, waiting for you. Up in the attic. Didn't you know?"

I weave my way slowly upstairs to bed, leaving him stupefied by my confessional torrent, too drunk to comprehend the depth of my pain. I'll pack tomorrow. *I Know Where I'm Going*, just like Wendy Hiller going back to Roger Livesey in the Powell and Pressburger film. And I know who's *not* going with me.

Chapter Eight

Je ferai un domaine
Où l'amour sera roi, où l'amour sera loi
Où tu seras reine.
Ne me quitte pas, ne me quitte pas, ne me quitte pas,
ne me quitte pas.

Jacques Brel, NE ME QUITTE PAS

So this is it. I've done it. They're downstairs together now, alone. I've done it, I've actually done it. I lie in my little bed under Nan's pink quilt in the dark, listening to the wind picking up outside, feeling like I couldn't sleep in a million years. I can hardly believe what's happened. I've found him. I've found Scott Walker, on Holy Island! It's all there, in the book. Scott Walker loved this Belgian singer, Jacques Brel. Just like Jack. Scott Walker sang this song about how he wanted to be "Jackie". Scott Walker was fond of whisky, just like Jack. Scott Walker was weird. This book says so. And American. And had fair hair. They've got the same nose. It's him.

And now she's downstairs with Scott Walker and any minute now he'll tell her who he is, or she'll look at him – properly, I mean, for the first time – and realise, and it'll be magic, and my dad will disappear from her head and she'll be happy again and I will have made it all right. For all of us. Me and Mum. Jack and Mum. Or should I say Scott and Mum? Happy ever after. Tonight's the night. They went out together after we went to bed. Where did they go? Have they been kissing on the beach under the moon, like in a Mills and Boon? Now they're back, together in the living-room. They're on the sofa together, or on the rug, they're doing it.

I'm smiling into the blackness, curled up under the bedclothes, imagining the future with me and him and Mum somewhere maybe abroad and she'll be holding his arm in the sunshine and laughing and he'll be grinning, although he hardly ever does, but when he falls in love with Mum he'll smile more than he ever has done in the past and he'll talk to us about those times when girls chased him in the street and she'll talk about the times when she was one of those girls and I'll listen and know that I brought them together, me, on my own – well, a bit of help from Nanbread, but basically me.

Then I hear footsteps coming up the stairs beneath me and I lie completely still, my heart thudding, listening.

It's Mum. She stumbles halfway up and mumbles something, then I hear her door open and then it closes again and I can hear the *thud-thud* as she drops her shoes and I'm so tense I feel as if I'm about to burst and then I hear it – the living-room door opening again and then heavier footsteps. Jack. Here he comes.

Oh my God. Please please please let him go into her room. Please. My whole body is waiting, blood pounding.

He pauses on the landing, it seems like forever.

I screw up my eyes and pray, and then I hear it – footsteps again only this time they're coming up to *me*, getting closer, he's coming up to the attic, he's coming here – and the door opens as I lean over and click on my bedside lamp and it's the most horrible brain-jangling moment in my entire life because Jack is standing there, hand on the door, staring at me. And I know what he wants. In that sickening crunching second I see he wants me, he wants what they all want, he wants to make with the big stick. With me.

The look on my face in that second must have told him everything because he backs out of the room almost as quickly as he arrived, and then the door's shut and I can hear the footsteps descending and then he's gone, the front door banging shut and silence. I don't care where he's gone, I hope it's the deepest pit of hell. I'm sick to my stomach with disgust. I could puke. I feel the vile taste rising up in my stomach and I switch off the light, a great horrified yawning hole where my mind should be.

I don't sleep. I lie there watching the pale sun slowly filter through the attic window. There's nothing left. Everything is ugly, everything stinks.

I hear Nan get up and wait for her to go out. It seems forever. I hear the birdwatchers from room five get up and I lie there listening to them yabbering to Nan in the kitchen about the difference between Eiders and Shelducks. Then they leave. Nan's clattering about doing washing-up and singing 'Ol' Man River' and the rest of the house is dead as a dodo. I wish they *were* dead. All of them. I don't want to think about it.

I think about Oombe instead and wonder where she is right now this minute and if she remembers me or did she make friends with Kelly Stevenson the moment I went and are they even now meeting by the tube station or going off to Tesco's to nick Bounty bars. The front door slams. Nan's gone to the shop. I get up and stick yesterday's clothes on and go downstairs. No one about. I take a piece of bread for breakfast and I'm out the back door and over the fence into the field and away down Sandham Lonnen towards Castlehead Rocks only it's raining, just a bit at first and then more and I get really wet because I didn't put a coat on or anything but I'm just going to keep walking because I don't know what else to do and I've got to stop my brain from having these thoughts that are crowding in, and being wet and walking keeps everything at bay because I have to concentrate on the rain dripping from my hair into the back of my neck and my cold wet feet and the blinding rain.

Suddenly my trudging is blocked by three pairs of feet. I look up. It's those wankers again. Baz, Paulie and The Sniffer.

"She's crying," one of them says. I try to walk past them, but they're not letting me.

"Fuck off," I say, not looking up. Rain, tears, it's all the same.

"I've got a deal to offer you," Baz says. He's standing with his collar up, like he's a detective or something.

"I don't do deals."

"You want some speed?"

They know how to stop me in my tracks, I'll say that for them.

"Why? You got some?"

Baz is shouting above the rain. "No, but I can get it . . . "

I walk on, briskly. "Yeah. Sure . . . " This time they let me go.

"We get it for you, – you have to pay us – in kind," he yells after me.

What a wozzer. "Of course," I shout back, still walking, my feet splashing in a lake-like puddle spreading across the lane. "Fine by me. You get the whizz, I'm yours."

Like they're going to get me drugs and I'm going to be their sex slave. What planet do they live on?

"Slag!" the little weedy one shouts after me as an afterthought.

I climb up away from them, sliding in the soaking grass, towards the castle garden. It's empty, the roses sagging under the rain. Standing on the slippery wall I can see the boys trailing back to the Donalds' farm, and I can see ducks on the farm pond and of course sheep standing stock still in the deluge, and Nan, under her red umbrella. She's heading away from the shop with her string bag full of shopping, and she's marching towards the West Field, below me. I wonder if she's gone a bit nuts, wandering about in the rain in the middle of nowhere. Maybe it's me. Or Mum. We've finally sent her round the twist.

"Joanna."

He's come up behind me without me hearing him, standing still, his face saying I don't know what, but unshaven. I turn away from where Nan is wandering below and jump off the wall. I hate him.

"You'll get pneumonia, standing out here," he says. His voice is cool, like last night didn't happen. Only I know it did, and so does he. I won't look at him. Instead I watch beads of rain racing down the gatepost. I can hear him unlocking the gate. Then he walks away towards his shed, and I hear the clink of his key as he turns it in the padlock.

It's like a monsoon out here. We did them in geography. The ditch below the castle is swelling and the rain is flooding down my face and drenching every inch of me. I follow Jack to the shed.

Inside he's put a kettle on the primus stove. Now he's moving flowerpots about, stacking them into dusty heaps. He won't look at me. I sit on a pile of sacks.

"You're Scott Walker, aren't you," I say finally.

The shifting of the flowerpots carries on. "Who?"

Oh, yes. Very clever. "Scott Walker," I say loudly. "Real name Noel Scott Engel. Born in Hamilton, Ohio. Came to England in nineteen sixty-five."

He has stopped with the pots. I look at him. He's staring at me. I look away again, quickly.

"*Who?*" he says.

I used to like him. He was the only person I could talk to. Now he's a traitor and a liar and a dirty old man. I get up, leaving a damp patch on the sacks.

"You wanker," I say. Then I leave. He doesn't follow me.

I squelch my way back down the hill to where I can see Billy's bus sitting by the bus stop, engine idling, waiting to cross over the causeway. He's reading the *Morning Star*, I can see him at the wheel through the blur of the windscreen. I bang on the bus door and it opens with a hiss.

"Hurry, lass," he says, "It's brass monkeys out there. Who'd believe it's August?"

I go to the back, as far away from him as possible. He doesn't ask me for the fare. The bus starts up. I'm going to Berwick to revisit my old mate Charlie Heaton. I'll probably have to do stuff to get some dope out of him, but I don't care. I really don't. I don't care about anything.

* * *

LILIE FERRARI

They've all gone a bit peculiar. Nan keeps staring at me as if I'm a Martian, asking me if I've got anything I want to tell her, looking at me like I'm Myra Hindley or something. I feel dirty, as if she knows I had to give Charlie a blow-job to get anything out of him. She looks at me like I'm disgusting. Which I am. Mum comes downstairs with her bag packed and talks about leaving, only the tide table doesn't fit in with the train or bus times till Thursday, and she bursts into tears and goes on about someone called the exterminating angel. She doesn't even remember to tell me to pack my things, she's so upset. She's pouring herself an early snifter in the kitchen and she suddenly stops and says *"Prairie Fire!"* in this excited voice.

"Pardon?" says Nan, ladling stewed apple out of a pan.

"Nothing," says Mum. "It was a magazine. A radical magazine."

"Should I have read it?" Nan is looking at her, those sharp little eyes like a mouse.

Mum shakes her head. "No . . . " Then she takes another swig of her drink. "Fancy that . . . " she murmurs. *"Prairie Fire."*

I'm telling you, they're both losing it. Me as well. I spent a day smoking Charlie's measly bit of dope and floating about, and now I'm so bored I could scream the house down. Nan cooking like a maniac because she says cooking apples wait for no man, they have to be cooked the moment they're picked and she's got a ton of them

178

sitting in buckets in the shed. Apple flan. Apple crumble. Apple tart. Apple dumplings. Apple turnovers. Mum is just waiting to get the fuck out of here. She won't really speak to me properly, just gets irritable and gets busy doing something if I ask her about Dad and going home.

I don't know what I want any more. I go walking round the island like I've done so many many times, only I avoid the garden, which is a shame because I miss it, I liked sitting in there on the bench facing the sundial, which says 'A Timely Reminder' on it; I liked watching the bees buzzing drunkenly round the roses, and the shadows getting longer and the distant tiny figures of people looking out of the castle windows and the sea crashing on the beach beyond Bibly Hill.

I toil up and down the dunes. I go out to Emmanuel Head, where a great white pyramid sits as a warning to ships about the rocks. There are rabbits everywhere. I walk from Chare Ends along the old Pilgrims' Way, following the wooden poles out into the bright hard shallows, the sun glimmering on the sea, the silhouettes of horses galloping across the mud flats. I stand and watch a man in a kilt playing the bagpipes alone in Coves Bay. I stare out from the Heigh at the gaunt black towers of Bamburgh Castle on the mainland, with grey and blue hills behind. Nan calls them the Cheviots. There's the ruin of a cottage up here, heaps of old bricks piled up. I wonder who lived there and why the house fell down. I hear a noise below, on the beach, and go to the edge, looking down onto the shingle. Jack's there, carrying planks of wood from the old lifeboat house round the corner. If he sees me he doesn't show it.

I go slowly down the steep path to the beach and follow him. If he says anything, I'll tell him to fuck off. He's there with the Redpaths and one of the old geezers who goes fishing, and they're standing about measuring and hammering. They're trying to repair the shack by the Herring Houses. I sit on a lobster pot and watch. John Redpath nods at me with his mouth full of nails, and the old fisherman grins and says something to me which sounds friendly, but I can't understand, his accent's too strong, so I don't smile back. Apart from that no one takes any notice of me. Least of all Jack.

I stay there for a few hours, just watching. I can't help it. It's Scott Walker hammering nails in. Probably shitting himself because I've found him, scared I'll phone the *Sunday People*, like the book says happened to him before when he was trying to hide. The sun's shining and there's no wind, and it's nice sitting here watching him and hugging my secret. Our secret. Finally they pack up for the day and head for the pub. Jack doesn't look back once.

The next day I go down there again, and this time he's on his own. I stand there waiting for him to say something, only he's struggling with this great big bit of wood and I can't just let him do it on his own, can I, so I go and help him carry it. He just says "Thanks," and then:

"Could you just hold onto that end while I fix this in place?" And I find myself doing it, like it's the most natural thing in the world.

So I help him with his building. I get up in the mornings, which shocks old Nanbread and I wear some horrible baggy jeans Mum packed for me when we left London in a hurry – I wouldn't be seen dead in them on Seven Sisters Road, but I don't care here. Then I go down to the Herring Houses and Jack's there smoking a roll-up and looking at the wooden framework we're building and deciding what to do next. Sometimes the old fishermen come and help, or John Redpath, and they don't say anything about me or why I'm there, just call me "hinny" like Nan does and when there's tea going they bring me a mug.

He's got everything left in the world stuffed into an old backpack and he sleeps in a sleeping bag in the least damaged bit of the shack and makes tea on a little primus stove like the one he's got in his shed. All his Jacques Brel CDs got burnt.

It's weird. I feel different about Jack now I know he's really Scott. Like he's here, in front of me, but I know he's lived another life. Before I was born. We never talk about when he came into my room. Sometimes Baz and his divvy mates watch us from up on the Heigh. They either hide and peer out over the gorse bushes, or else they stand up and shout things. I know what's going on – Baz is getting angry but he doesn't know why. I do. He can't understand why I should be making the big stick with this old guy – which is what he thinks I'm doing – but not fucking him. After all, he's seventeen, not too spotty. He so wants me to fancy him, and he's so furious because I don't.

Anyway, one night I've fetched Jack and me fish and chips from the van that comes over on Thursdays, tides permitting, and we're sitting together in the half-built house, not talking, just finishing our chips. The house isn't ready yet, but the window's back in, and there's a brand new wall growing every day. A tarpaulin pulled over the gaping hole above where the roof should be keeps the tools dry and the rain out. We sit in silence, listening to the surge of the sea. Tonight there are a million stars out there, and the shadow of the castle with the moon sailing fast across the black, gusty sky. Jack sees I've finished and takes my chip papers away and puts them in the old rusty bin he's using as a stove. He drops a match in, and there's a quick flare of brightness. I can see his face quite clearly as he sits down again. We don't say a word. Just us, sitting there. I want to feel like I used to, only I can't, because I know what he thinks about me, he thinks like they all do, only I'm confused and embarrassed and excited all at once. That's the difference. I know he's just another dirty old sod, but a bit of me wants that, wants him to do things to me. The things my dad did.

I get up suddenly. "Got to go," I say, my voice sounding stupid and gruff.

I know he thinks this is peculiar, because usually I stay and have some of his revolting black instant coffee before I go; but he just looks and says "Okay."

I can see the gleam of his eye in the faltering flame from the stove. My legs turn to jelly.

"Goodnight," he says. His eye is steady.

Abruptly, I walk away, my heart pounding, my face ridiculously red. I feel as if something is – was – about to happen between me and Jack. I mean Scott. If I had wanted it to. And I don't know what I think about that any more. I just know I have to get out of there, to walk away in the dark with the wind singing against my cheeks and taste the moment before it goes.

I can't go home. I head out towards the West Field, hardly knowing what I'm doing, Scott Walker songs in my head and Jack's face swimming in front of my eyes and the memory of Dad and what he did and what a mess I am, what a dirty little slag I am, and then I hear it. A whimper. I don't believe. Can't believe it. I start to stumble towards the sound.

It's the dog – still here, in the sheep-pen where I left it, but not tied up, not dying like I've imagined. A little maggot-infested skeleton, that's what I thought it'd be by now. I feel its ribs. It's a bit skinny and more than a bit crazy, but not dying. It's also insanely happy to see me and jumps all over me, suffocating me with stupid dog affection. I push it off and shout at it. It sits in the dark, watching me with a bright eye, waiting to see what I'll do next. For a golden second I see myself letting the dog go, taking it home with me, being its friend, me and Jack and the dog together.

I'm standing there staring at it when a hand touches me on the shoulder and I nearly jump out of my skin. I whip round, and it's Baz, leaning over the wall of the pen. I might have guessed.

"Piss off, creep," I say, tense about the dog and Jack and everything. "Why are you always following me? Go home and have a wank."

I can't see his face, just the whiteness of his hands resting on the stones. I move out of the pen away from the dog and shut the gate. Baz is standing in front of me now, and I can see him. He's grinning. "You let everyone else have a bit," he says. "My turn."

"Where's the speed, then?" I ask. The dog makes a little sad noise and I walk away quickly, Baz right on my heels, so close I can feel his breath on my shoulder. He hasn't got any speed, of course. He wants something in advance, he says. A down payment. I'm weighing up how much I should do. Just enough to keep him interested, but not enough so that I don't get my speed, if by some miracle he ever actually gets his hands on any, and I decide a quick wank should do the trick, and I turn and look at him, and at the very moment I think my mind's made up and I'm about to touch him, it hits me, like one of those thunderbolts you get in those coloured pictures in the school bibles. It's what Nan's been harping on about all this time. *I don't have to do this*. I don't have to do it just because I know how to, because it won't take long and you never know I might get something out of it. If I don't want to, I don't have to.

Miss Super Casual. "No thanks," I say, walking off. There's a short moment when I think I've left him standing there, but no, he's behind me again, I can hear his feet in the grass echoing mine.

"Come on," he says, "Stop pissing about. You know you're gagging for it."

"Fuck off."

"I'm on my own. The other two went to Berwick. I won't tell them if you don't want me to. It could just be you and me, secret."

"Fuck off. Tosser."

"I'm serious."

"So am I."

I keep walking, annoyed and pleased with myself all at once. I can hear his feet crushing the long grass, dogging me. We're heading for the dunes. I just want to think about Jack. Scott. I'm getting irritated. I stop suddenly, so suddenly that Baz nearly bumps into me. He's panting, a little out of breath.

"Listen," I say, calm. "I don't fancy you, all right? I think you're an oily twat. And I don't want your little tiny dinger anywhere near me. I'd rather eat shit than fuck you."

He tries to grab my arm but I pull away and start walking again.

"You've been gagging for it for weeks," he says, "Creaming your pants every time I see you. Go on. Deny it."

I laugh. "I deny it." He's still coming after me. He grabs my arms and twists them behind my back.

"Slapper," he says into my ear. "Dirty little cow." He's hurting me, nails digging into my wrists, and I feel the sting of twisted skin as I struggle to free myself and he hangs on. It's a silent little fight, but he's strong – all that work on the Donalds' farm, he can couple a trailer to a tractor all on his own, I've seen him, and now he's got me so tight against him, my arms bent back, I struggle to speak.

"Let go –"

He's pushing me downwards, until I can't resist any more, and my knees hit the grass. But I'm not scared. I've been in worse situations. And anyway, he hasn't got the guts to do anything.

And all the time he's calling me names and trying to kiss me, and I keep thinking – why would you want to kiss someone you hate? And I'm pulling my face away, screwing up my lips, and I have a brainwave and gather up a great gob of spit and aim it at him as his face closes in and then it all changes and he hits me so hard in the face that I see bright colours spinning in front of me and then I'm on the ground and he's hurting me now, forcing his rough hand up my leg, then he's on top of me and struggling with his jeans and then he's inside and I'm trying to push him away and I can hear a deep groaning noise and it's me, swallowing sobs that come down from inside of me and he's pushing and hurting and not caring what he's doing, not a person any more, not a human being, just moving, grunting, no mind. Down here in the spiky grass it's Gaby all over again, *papa, non, pas ça, pas ça* . . . no say in the matter just shut up and shut your eyes and let him get on with it. All the time I can hear the dog, shut in the pen and whining, scrabbling at the bricks. I remember then, the dog shut in the cupboard in London, the same thing then, the same thing now.

It's over really quick. I lie there, feeling the wetness of him on my legs. He rolls off me. I can hear the wind through the grass and the dog whining. Shuffling about zipping up his flies, he's sitting up on one elbow and saying something about how I can be his girlfriend now, we can be friends, that it's all right really. There's a blackness in front of my eyes.

I get up somehow. I can't see him. I stagger away towards the sound of the sea and away from the yelping of the dog, more frantic now, hoarse barking, like it knows I'm going away. I can hear the waves crashing on the shingle, it's getting louder, and above the sound I can hear Baz yelling my name in the darkness, following me, scared. He's behind me all the time. My feet hit the beach and I can see the great black wall of water ahead and he's shouting behind me, trying to explain his actions, trying to say we can be friends, anything. I feel the water closing around me like a cold hand and he's splashing behind me, crying now, sobbing for me to come back. I keep walking into the icy clasp of the swell, so cold it makes me gasp, and he's suddenly right behind me and grabbing at me and we struggle together, shouting obscenities into the raging dark and swallowing salt water and then I pull away and swim out into the deep, letting myself be pulled by the waves and then tossed back again, over and over until I don't know which way is up or which is the sea and which the sky, and I don't hear his voice any more so I gasp and struggle upwards until my lungs are bursting and I get a sudden glimpse of moon-whitened sand and I head back to what I know is the shore, swimming for my life until I feel the shingle grazing my hands. I stagger onto the beach and collapse, the breath knocked out of me.

I am a blank, black nothing. I open my eyes and there's someone peering down at me, pulling strands of wet hair from my face.

"Are you all right?"

It's Billy, the old geezer, of all people. I'm so surprised I start to smile.

"Where's your bus?" I ask weakly.

"We better get you home, pet," he says. "Can you sit up?"

I lie there weakly, convinced my legs are broken. He's squatting down next to me, as if he's got all the time in the world. "Bit of a night-bird, aren't you," he says conversationally. "Your nan was worried. Sent me out to look for you."

I wonder fleetingly if he found the dog on his way. I haul myself up to a sitting position and immediately feel the rush of sour water exploding from my guts. He holds my shoulders as I vomit water onto the sand.

"Funny time for a swim," he says when it's over.

I wipe my hand across my mouth and look at him. I can see suddenly what a kind man he is. And I remember what I decided: *I don't have to do this*. Only I had.

I touch his arm. He looks at me, surprised. "I was raped," I say and start to cry.

* * *

All hell's broken loose. I've spent the dawn with Nan asking me questions and Mum white-lipped and not speaking and at the whisky far too early, and then the tide went out and the causeway opened and now the police are here, and I've told them over and over it was Baz but they keep going away and coming back and saying he's not at the farm and no one can find him, am I sure he isn't away with the other two lads having a weekend off in Berwick, that's what Mr Donald said.

They're waiting for a doctor to come and they've taken my clothes away in plastic bags and told me not to wash, although one of them says it's a waste of time because I've been in the sea, and I'm shivering all over in

LILIE FERRARI

Nan's red quilted dressing-gown and I'm so tired I just
want to sleep but they won't let me, keep telling me a
rape counsellor's coming with the doctor. Only I don't
need a rape counsellor, do I, I need a bit of peace and
quiet, and I keep worrying about Jack, he'll be wondering
where I've got to and why I'm not there helping him with
the door frame like I said I would.

There's a moment when Nan's in the kitchen with
Billy making the police some tea and I'm left alone for
the first time with Mum, who's hardly said anything since
Nan woke her up. She stands staring out of the window
through the net curtains onto the street as if she expects
something to happen out there. She's smoking a
cigarette.

"Give us one, Mum . . . "

She turns and glares at me, and then to my amazement
throws the packet at me, so hard it hits me on the
shoulder and hurts and I yelp in surprise. It's followed by
the household box of matches she's been holding and it
just misses me and hurtles to the carpet.

"Go on," she says savagely. "You might as well."

I'm a bit shocked by her tone. I retrieve the matches
and light the cigarette, scared. She's more angry than
even that night when she walked in and found me and
Dad on the sofa.

"I hope you're happy," she says. She's staring at me
now. "I hope you're bloody happy."

I don't say anything. I don't know what she means. My

190

heart is pounding in my chest, it feels like it's going to burst out through the red quilting.

"You've got what you wanted, haven't you? All the attention you need."

I hear myself saying in a small sullen little voice that I didn't want attention, she's wrong – but she interrupts.

"He put you up to this, didn't he?"

"Who?"

"Don't play the little innocent, Joanna. You know very well who."

"I don't –"

"That cowboy friend of yours, calls himself Jack. Although of course that isn't his name."

She starts pacing up and down in front of me, smoking like a maniac, not looking at me. "He's clever, I'll give him that . . . " She stops suddenly and stands looking down at me. Instinctively I draw my knees up under me in the protective tent of Nan's dressing-gown. "He told you, didn't he?" she says. It's not a question, it's a statement. She's like a raving loony standing there. I can see her hand shaking, the one holding the fag.

"Told me what?"

"That I'm going back to London."

She really has lost her marbles. "Mum," I say wearily, "I know we're going back. All the business with the trains and the tide tables, remember?" It's all the booze, sending her doolally.

"No," she says, "you didn't hear me. I said I was going

back. Not you. Me. On my own. And I told him – that Yank. I told him that in confidence and he told you, didn't he? So you have to come up with this bit of bad soap opera to put the kybosh on my plans –"

I sit there, shivering and shocked and speechless while she rants on about Jack, about how everything's his fault, in fact if I've had sex with anyone she says, it's probably him. I'm like a zombie, not hearing what she's saying. My mum was going to leave me. She was going to go back to Dad and leave me.

It's all a blur after that. There's a babble of voices and other people in the room and I'm trying to deny what she's saying about Jack but no one believes me, not Billy, not Gran, most of all not my mum. It all makes sense, I can hear them saying: she's had a crush on him for weeks, and she's been with him all the time, and I hear Mum telling them about the night she sat downstairs with him and how he obviously had the hots for me and it's disgusting I'm just a kid. *Oh yes, mum, just a kid when it suits you.* If there's been a rape, I hear her saying, then the prime candidate for rapist is Jack Dalton, or whatever his real name is.

Then Nan is suddenly alone with me in the room and she grabs me by the arm and pulls me upstairs, saying sod the doctor, she's not waiting, and she makes me stand in the cold cleanness of her bare little bedroom and take the dressing-gown off and show her all my body. She studies the scratches on my arms and looks at me.

"These are claw marks," she says slowly. I tell her Baz must have done it, but she just looks at the scratches the dog made and says nothing. She goes downstairs.

A policeman calls up to ask if I'm all right, something about detectives coming, and I shout down in my best normal voice that I'm just going to have a pee and then I lock myself in the bathroom and stand under the shower and scrub myself quickly until my skin is bright red, shoving the flannel right up inside me, sluicing him out of my body. I don't care any more. It doesn't matter about evidence. No one believes me anyway.

I tiptoe out of the bathroom and creep upstairs to my attic, where I pull on some clothes under the calm eyes of Scott Walker on the wall and then I tiptoe down and wait on the landing until I hear them. They've moved to the front room with the tea tray and the Hobnobs and I creep down like someone committing a crime in *Ironside* and get out via the back door.

The air smells good. I feel as if I've been locked in the house for weeks. I take great lungfuls as I head down towards the harbour and the Herring Houses. There he is, cool in the centre of my chaos, smoking a spliff and listening to Radio Four. I hate to do this, but I have to. There's only him now.

"Hi," he says, looking up. "Sleep late?"

I tell him about Baz, about the rape. I call it rape, and when I get to the word, Jack looks at me, and I see it. I see that he believes me. He extinguishes the joint with his brown fingers and shoves it back into the tin with the orange mountain on it. I finish telling him, about the police and the rape counsellor coming and Mum saying she's sure it was him who raped me.

He stands up slowly, thinking. Then for the first time ever he touches me and I feel my whole body tingle. All he does is squeeze my shoulder.

"You'll have to go back, Joanna," he says in that dark, serious voice. "And I'll have to go."

Go? Go? He can't go!

"I know what's going to happen," he says. "I'm the outsider in this place. I'm going to get the blame. Plus –" and his eyes slide away from mine – "your mom knows something about me. And she's likely to tell people."

So now I know. He really is Scott.

"We'll run away together," I say, trying to grab hold of his hand, but he pulls it away.

"No," he says. "No. Absolutely not." He picks up his old backpack from the corner. He looks at me, a long look.

"Goodbye," he says.

And then he's gone, striding away across the shingle, not looking back. I stand shocked for a second, but then I realise I can't let him do this, I can't let him go without me, and I run outside. He's climbing the hill towards the priory, over to the causeway side of the island. I follow him quietly, creeping along hiding behind bushes, ducking down behind dry stone walls, tiptoeing so as not to disturb the sheep. As Jack reaches the market-place I can hear the siren of a police car racing towards us, and Jack disappears into the bus shelter as it passes. We're on Chare Ends now, I can see the sea and the posts on the Pilgrims Way and some children plod past me in sunhats carrying a bucket full of crabs. Jack is striding across the sand, taking the shortest route, exposed on the windy beach. I'm a way behind him, darting from post to post, when he suddenly whips round and sees me. I call to him, but my voice is taken away on the wind. He turns back towards the oncoming sea and starts running. I begin to weep. I run as well, but I can't catch him. He's going to shake me off.

I keep running and shouting and crying right up to him, up to the water's edge, where Jack is standing, the toecaps of his boots in the small circling shallows.

"It's no good," he says. "We're too late."

We both shade our eyes and look across at the marker pole further out in the water. He's right – the water's risen above the line. We can't get across. We're stuck on the island.

He starts walking away from me, along the water's edge, back towards the village. "Go away," he says.

I don't say anything, just keep up. "I'm leaving in the morning," he says, his eyes looking somewhere into the distance, "the moment the tide's out."

"Good," I say. "We could catch the early bus to Alnwick and then get a train." He's making me puffed out, walking so fast.

"Joanna. You're going back home."

I feel the tears coming again. "I'm not."

"You are."

"I'll kill myself."

"Don't be stupid."

I stop walking. "You don't believe me?"

He turns and looks back at me. He seems suddenly much older, and just for a scary second I wonder what I'm doing, but I have no options. What else is there to do? In the distance there are gulls screaming, following a fishing boat out to the open sea. I feel very small then, and suddenly not able to do this, any of it. I'm exhausted. I sit down on the sand, shaking. I could do with some *khat* now. What a long way off all of that life now is. I'm turning into Lorna McKenzie. Jack's feet are planted in front of me.

"Come on," he says.

We go to the garden, of course. Now the causeway's closed no one will come there. We sit on the bench in silence by the sundial and watch the shadows lengthen along the little gravel paths. There's something wonderful about sitting in that garden with the gate locked and Jack having the key. The secret garden. I keep thinking *this is what it feels like, to have a mother who doesn't want you.*

After a while Jack tells me I've got my whole life ahead of me. People over the age of about twenty are always making that speech. It really bugs me. Who's to say you can't be fourteen and feel like there's no future to speak of? He tells me I've got to go back and face the music. He says he'll take me. We're busy arguing when we hear a police siren, very loud, somewhere close. I go cold. Over beyond the back wall of the garden, below us on the beach, there's something happening. I can see people moving about in the fading light, and faint shouts coming on the wind. Jack goes to the shed and gets out his binoculars. He stands on the bench and squints through them for a long while, then he steps down and looks at me.

"I think they've found Baz," he says, a peculiar expression on his face. He hands me the binoculars.

Someone is tying orange tape to road-traffic cones down there, and there's an ambulance, and a little tent. And two men in wetsuits standing over something. A body, not moving, covered in what looks like dust until I realise it's sand. Jack's right. I recognise the clothes. I hand the binoculars back.

"He shouldn't have come after me," I say, and then I'm sick, violently, into a bed of pink poppies.

We sleep in the shed, together on the pile of sacks, him and me. This is the best night of my life so far. His arm round me, keeping me safe, but no sex at all, no groanings, no stirrings, just his calm in the eye of my storm. I try to stay awake because I'm scared he'll wait until I'm asleep then sneak off. But I can't fight it. The warm dark closes in.

Chapter Nine

Bless O Lord this island,
This Holy Island.
Make it a place of peace and love.
Make it a place of joy and light.
Make it a place of holiness and hospitality.
Make it a place of grace and goodness
And begin with me.

Canon David Adam, PRAYER OF ST AIDAN

I was up all night waiting for Joanna to come home. I used the time to sort out jars and write labels for chutney-making. They found that boy's body washed up all bruised and battered by the rocks down below the castle. Once I'd organised the jars into stacks and put them into the larder, I went back into the sitting-room and started on the jumper I had decided to knit for

Joanna for when winter came. The girl didn't have a single warm item of clothing to her name. It was a nice Aran – complicated but rewarding. I chose black wool, because I knew that's the only shade she would contemplate being seen in; although a lovely vivid red would have been far better with her complexion. I had been telling the police – and myself – that Joanna's disappearance was just a muddle-headed girl running off into the night. She couldn't go far, the tide was in, and anyway she knew the island like the back of her hand. She wasn't going to go tumbling over the cliffs. But there was a dead body now. It changed everything.

I didn't know which boy it was at first. They just talked about it being one of the lads working at the Donalds' Farm. But then they started to describe him. Tall. Dark hair. It was the one Joanna had sent packing, the one Jack Dalton had a tussle with at Martha's wedding. I began to worry even more for Joanna then. Cath began to droop and doze around three o'clock, and I sent her up to bed. I said I'd wake her if there was any news. I don't know whether I meant it or not, to be honest. She was so addled with the booze there seemed little point in involving her. So I sat in my armchair concentrating on my casting-on while the young policewoman sat opposite, her head drooping, waking up every now and then when static crackled on her radio and distant voices barked incomprehensible police business.

In the space of one evening the police presence on the island had expanded, gone from being one chap and the young Amis girl, pink-faced and sweating in her new constable's uniform (her parents live in Belford), to a gaggle of grim-faced detectives from Berwick. They were in the kitchen. I got up at one point to make sure I hadn't left the immersion on, and found them poring over a big map of the island, which they'd got spread out on the kitchen table. They all straightened up when I came in and looked embarrassed. I knew what they were doing. They were looking to see how many places a girl might throw herself into the sea.

I checked the immersion. It was off. "She'll be back," I said firmly. They didn't answer. They had sent a squad car out looking for her earlier, but then it got dark and they gave up. Billy had left before teatime, he had to drive the bus, do the Berwick run. He wanted to stay but I told him not to be so stupid. No reason for him to lose his job.

I saw him out into the hall. He kissed me clumsily on the cheek and I wished he hadn't, not in front of all these strangers.

"See you first thing in the morning," he said. "I'll change my shift – I'll be back by dawn."

"Don't be daft," I said. His eagerness was beginning to stretch my patience. He began to tell me a story then, something about a girl he remembered, when he was a lad in Christon Bank. "Just walked into the Blinkbonny

Arms," he said. "Stark naked, she was. Mad. Not a stitch on." I stared at him, wondering why he was telling me this. He shifted a little, uncomfortable on the hall rug. "Young girls," he said. "Like hares in spring. Unpredictable . . . "

So I spent the night knitting in the armchair I've sat in for the past twenty years, and I had a lot of time to think, staring into the electric fire listening to the wind outside. The tide was in; we were cut off from the outside world. I kept trying to imagine what it must be like to be Cath at this moment, lying upstairs wondering if her daughter was dead or alive; but oddly, I couldn't imagine what she must be feeling or thinking. I suppose it was because I knew she'd probably be thinking nothing at all, feeling nothing, her head full of booze-flavoured dreams. I tried then to think about my other children: little dead Alice; Jessie and Mary, the twins; Tom, David, John. What was the other one called? I couldn't remember. Somehow when I thought about my children, my living children, they merged in my memory into one demanding, screeching, jam-coloured angry little face. I suppose I hadn't been a wonderful mother, not like the magazines are always telling you to be. I wasn't there when they came home from school, I never asked them about their homework. There seemed to be no real connection, apart from the fact they all had Tommy's hair.

The Amis girl had really nodded off now. So much for all her training courses. Wasn't she supposed to be counselling me, being a support in my hour of need? There was bound to be a chapter on people in my situation in her police manual. Still, I couldn't blame her. She seemed drained by the drama of the day. Poor bairn. Probably never expected to be dealing with a murder, not when she was only three weeks out of the training school. Anyway, nothing was going to happen, not till morning, when the tide went out and the sun rose; and then we would know. I shook the thought away. To distract myself from the creeping fear that stiffened my bones as I sat there, I tried then to think about my grandchildren – the other ones, the ones that weren't Joanna – but that was worse. I remembered the ones who had come from Australia, with their whiny accents and their loud, exhausting energy, but not their names. Just thinking about them all made me weary. But Joanna – I could remember things she had said, her sharp little observations, the way she dragged her feet across the hall carpet, her frown. I think I fell asleep then, and was woken by the sound of the wind rattling a dustbin lid outside. The beginnings of pale light glimmered behind the curtains. It was almost morning.

Quietly I got up, taking care not to drop any stitches or disturb the girl, and tiptoed out to the hall. I could hear the detectives murmuring in the kitchen, and the sound of the kettle chuntering away on the range, about to boil. I slipped on my old coat and opened the front door. I hadn't locked it the previous night. Well, you lock your door against burglars and intruders, don't you? And I had half the Berwick police force snoozing in my kitchen. The wind hadn't dropped. Out towards the castle small pockets of mist still sat between the hillocks in the dim, damp light. The squad car was still parked out by my gate. A light was on in the post office, so I walked down the street and peered through the window. Jessie Bell was unloading packets of firelighters onto a shelf.

She heard me tapping on the window and crossed to unlock the door. It was still an hour before she opened for business.

"Eeh, Sylvie, pet," she said, drawing me inside, torn between nosiness and sympathy. "It's a nasty business, this."

"Not for you," I remarked. "All those police – they'll have bought your entire stock of Benson and Hedges before the day's out. Smoking themselves stupid in my kitchen. Five of them."

"She always looked like trouble, that one," Jessie said. "Far too knowing for her age. I blame the parents."

"A tin of Chum, please." She subsided then, hearing my frosty tone, and clattered off to fetch it, lips pursed. I couldn't blame her for what she said; she didn't know Joanna. It wasn't the words that upset me, it was the fact that she was already talking about my grandchild in the past tense, as if she was already dead.

I stepped back out onto Marygate. Up around the

castle now I could see small figures walking about in pairs. Only today they weren't tourists, they were islanders, searching for Joanna. I recognised the stout, squat figure of Ted Armstrong, beating his stick through the black shadow of nettles that bordered the car park; and with him, the stooped shoulders of another familiar figure – Micky Reid. He was unlocking the upturned boat sheds and peering inside. I wondered what he expected to find. A body? Billy's bus was parked by the castle entrance, and further up, I could see Billy, as good as his word, heading away from the others towards the garden, part of the search team. Up beyond the Lough, another searcher was climbing the stile onto the links. And everywhere there were the sheep, little more than ragged shapes in the half-light, cropping blindly at the grass, heads down, coats glistening still with a layer of dew, just as if it was an ordinary day.

"Mrs Weatherson?" PC Amis was standing at my elbow, huddled inside her thin police mac, trying to wake up. "You should have given me a shout."

I walked with her back to the house, not listening as she burbled on about everything possible being done, good men out there, let them do their job, how about a nice cup of tea. I pushed the tin of dog food deep into the pocket of my coat. Why do young people always imagine that just because we have wrinkled faces our minds have gone? I could have punched her. Tea, indeed.

We went back inside. "Is my daughter out of bed?" I

asked. There were two men in the hall. One was talking on a mobile phone. He turned to one side and spoke urgently into it, facing the wall when he saw me, avoiding my eyes. The Amis girl took my elbow and ushered me back into my own sitting-room. Someone had opened the curtains and the room looked cold and grubby in the light. Cath was sitting hunched over the fire, her hands round a mug of tea.

"No news," she said, hardly looking at me. I didn't reply. Those thin, freckled hands reminded me of Tommy. I went back to my knitting.

I could hear the man in the hall saying " Black jeans, blue t-shirt." Then a small silence. Then: "They're not sure. No one saw her leave. But those are the clothes that seem to be missing from her room."

Black jeans, blue t-shirt. *Crimewatch*. Last seen wearing black jeans and a blue t-shirt. They were usually dead, or else they just never came back.

I must have fallen asleep, because the next thing I knew I was knocked back into the armchair by something wet and yellow leaping onto my lap, covering my face and neck with slavering dog kisses, making small, loving, whimpering noises.

"Micky Reid found it," Billy said, standing uncomfortably in the doorway. "Down in the West Field."

I patted the dog and pushed it to the floor. "Good heavens," I said. "Good God." The dog lay on its back and exposed its soft belly, writhing and grinning, too happy to know how to behave.

Billy bent down to caress the dog. It responded with pathetic enthusiasm, licking his hand in a desperate, manic way, as if this might prevent some random act of cruelty. It was quivering with emotion.

"It was in the old sheep-pen. There was a plastic bowl full of water in there. And a couple of bones," said Billy. "Someone's been feeding it."

"I'll put the kettle on," I said, and headed for the kitchen. The dog followed, barking hoarsely with joy, its body bumping against my ankles.

There was the clatter of feet on the stairs and Cath appeared, red-eyed, excited. Her face fell at the sight of the dog wriggling by my feet.

"It's a miracle," I said. "Come on, now, fella. It's all right. You're home now."

"I'll get it some water," said the young policewoman, who had come in behind Cath, with Billy at her heels. "Is this Joanna's dog? You didn't mention a dog."

"It went missing weeks ago," Cath said. Billy was watching my face. I looked away, concentrating on the dog.

"So it wouldn't have been with Joanna –"

"No," I could hear myself, harsh.

"Any more news?" Cath lit a cigarette, her hand shaking. She was paler than usual, more ethereal, sober for once. I had never noticed before the thinness of her arms, pale and freckled, nor the gauntness of her neck.

The Amis girl shook her head, crouching over the

dog, looking up at Cath, her face fixed in a professional, caring expression. Tears spilled onto Cath's cheeks and she choked a little. "He's out there," she said. "A murderer."

"Jack Dalton? He's not a murderer," said Billy.

The policewoman had stood up again, and had an arm round Cath's bony shoulders.

"Billy . . . " I said, reproachfully. Now was not the time for island loyalty.

Cath turned on him, spitting out the words. "There's one kid already dead!" she said. "If there's one, why not two?" She crumpled, sobbing. The policewoman ushered her away.

Billy looked at me. His face was blank with shock. I realised that no one had told him. He'd got off his bus and just started searching for Joanna, as he'd promised.

"Joanna's dead?" he asked, confused.

"That tall boy from the Donald place," I said. "The one who had a scrap with Joanna at Martha's wedding. Washed up on the beach last night."

"Dead?" He was still caressing the dog, staring at me.

"His mother's coming from Morpeth to identify the body."

Billy sat down heavily at the table in the chair vacated by a detective, who slid out of the room, his mobile phone ringing shrilly.

"You look like you could do with a cuppa," I said. I stood at the sink, clattering crockery about, letting the water from the tap froth and gurgle over a bowlful of teacups the detectives had left. How many times had he sat and watched me there and I'd felt a comfortable feeling in my heart, as though this was where he was meant to be? Only now he looked at me and I didn't look back, and I felt a great distance between us.

"You don't seem very surprised about the dog coming back," he said finally. It had collapsed at my feet and was licking my shoe, its tail thrashing. It seemed half-mad, punch-drunk with freedom and relief.

"Damn!" I held up a cup. The handle had come off. I was almost weeping. It was the strain, you see. Joanna gone, and then Billy finding the dog.

"Put that down, hinny," he said. "You look done in. Get that lass in the uniform to do the tea."

I turned to him then, suddenly sure of the awful thought that had crept into the outer edges of my fear. "You stupid man," I said. "You stupid, stupid man. You've seen Jack, haven't you? You know where he is."

"I didn't know there was anyone dead," he said, his voice weak with excuses. "I just knew he wasn't a rapist, that's all."

He made to stand up and reach out to me, but I pushed him away sharply, causing him to stumble and stand on the dog, which let out a high-pitched yelp and leapt backwards, knocking over the compost bucket. I ran towards the door, calling for my daughter. Billy sat down in the chair again, trembling. He had made a mistake. He had made a bad mistake. A puddle was forming on the tiles, and a rancid, sour smell rose up, a mixture of rotting fruit, tea leaves and cooked vegetables. The dog began to eat the stinking mess with enthusiasm, wolfing the congealed heaps down in great, desperate gulps, as Cath appeared in the doorway, her face bright with expectation.

* * *

They kept Billy shut in the sitting-room, questioning him. Sometimes I could hear his voice raised, indignant, his tone defensive. Then they called the Amis girl out of the kitchen and there was a bit of excited muttering, and the slam of the front door. She came back, to where Cath and I sat at the kitchen table, to tell us that Billy had seen Joanna and Jack together, asleep in a garden shed in Gertrude Jekyll's walled garden, up by the castle. Cath leapt to her feet.

"I want to go," she said, her voice unnaturally loud after the long silence of our suspense. "Please."

PC Amis hesitated, looking at me and then at Cath, not sure what the rule book said about such a situation.

"Go on," I said. "I'll be fine. I'll wait. I'm too old for running about."

They left me alone, and I sat then, one hand on the dog's soft back, feeling the slow release of dread as it dissolved into relief. Joanna was alive. Joanna would get to wear the black Aran jumper. I got up and went to the hall, where I retrieved the tin of dog-food from my coat pocket.

"Here, lad," I said, "You didn't get your breakfast this morning, did you?"

I sat and watched him as he wolfed down the contents of the tin. His legs were trembling. It would be a while before he felt normal again. Me as well.

I waited for an hour, but no one came. Finally I went outside, and peered up the street towards the castle, but there was no sign of anyone up by the garden. I could see its grey walls quite clearly now that the sun was up and shining. A few seagulls wheeled above it, but not a human to be seen.

I went back inside and put on my coat. On an impulse I pulled Joanna's leather jacket from the hook. She'd be needing this, it was windy out there. I pushed the dog back into the hall and pulled the door closed behind me. As I walked away down the path I could hear it whimpering, its nose snuffling in the draught under the front door.

I headed out along Marygate, which seemed to be deserted. Then someone came puffing up behind me. It was the Verbena Hotels man, nasty little Dennis Bannion, incongruous in his suit.

"Want a lift? I've got the Range Rover."

I shook my head and kept walking. "Unsavoury business," he said, panting alongside me. I increased my pace in the vain hope of shaking him off. "Not good for tourist throughput."

I kept walking, my face expressionless, although inside I was battling with myself not to aim a good hard punch right between the man's eyes. But I'm too old for that sort of thing.

"I'll be spending tonight writing up a full report for head office," Bannion was saying as he unlocked his car. "But it doesn't look good. Definitely doesn't look good."

I paused and gazed for a second at my unwanted companion. "Just goes to show, lad – every cloud has a silver lining," I said.

I walked on alone to Chare Ends. A small crowd had gathered, staring out across the sands, engrossed in some distant drama. Jessie was there, and the Redpaths, and Jamie Lang. When they saw me they went quiet. I pushed my way through the people and began to walk across the sand, ignoring the road, taking the shortest possible route so that I could catch up with the posse of people who had congregated ahead of me. A helicopter was circling above, drowning out the sound of the seabirds and ruffling the red fronds of Cath's hair I could see in the distance.

I struggled through the sludge of sand, cursing my age and my slow, exhausted legs. Then I looked up and suddenly I could see Jack Dalton standing with Joanna on the road a short distance away. They were surrounded by police. It was hard to hear what was being said, but words floated across in the sharp sunlight, bouncing off the dazzle of the surrounding sea. A tired-looking man in a

red puffa jacket was talking to Jack about someone called
Barry Anderson, also known as Baz. I guessed it was the
boy from the farm. Joanna, a tiny figure, stood looking up
at the American, refusing to shift her gaze. I joined the
group of people nearby, who were standing back, as if
embarrassed by the drama of the spectacle, listening.
Billy was among them, and Cath. The helicopter floated
upwards for a moment, and I heard the American's voice,
broken, as I had never heard it before. Not that he ever
said much at the best of times, but now he was speaking.
Unexpected words. CIA. Crimes in America. Fugitive.
And then I saw that his eyes were wet and he was
mouthing one word, again and again. The word was
"guilty". The man – a detective, I supposed – shouted
back at him, and Jack shut up. Whatever the red-
jacketed man was saying had suddenly hit home. Jack
Dalton was being arrested under suspicion of the murder
of the work-experience boy from the Donald farm.

Then everyone moved and spoke at once. At some
signal, the helicopter rose and bobbed away to the
mainland. The red-jacketed man produced some
handcuffs and stepped towards Jack, who held his hands
out. He was staring at Joanna, speechless. I wanted to call
out to Joanna, but it wasn't the moment. Cath was there,
sobbing, trying to get between them. I had the impression
of a message flashing from Jack to Joanna, as a policewoman
took her arm, pulled her away. It seemed to me that
Joanna was about to say something important, and that

Jack Dalton had mutely told her to shut up. Joanna allowed herself to be drawn back, enduring the weeping and clutching of her mother, her eyes never leaving his face, accepting silently whatever it was he had told her with his eyes. *For once in her noisy little life she shuts up*, I thought.

I felt someone touch my arm. It was Billy. "Sylvie –" he said. I pushed him off and stepped forward to put the leather jacket round Joanna's shivering shoulders. She turned suddenly towards me, shoving her mother aside with a savage gesture. I held her a little, awkwardly, me and one skinny girl in the middle of all this, the child of my child, Tommy's blood coursing through her veins, connecting us.

A police car chugged forward and drew up beside us. I looked over Joanna's head at the crowd; they were murmuring, drawing back, the show almost over. No one could look at Jack. As he was about to lower his head and climb inside the car, he suddenly stopped and spoke to a policeman, said something briefly in a tired, low voice and struggled to remove something from his jeans pocket, which he handed over. Then he got into the back of the car with the man in the red jacket, the door slammed, and the car began to edge away towards the mainland. Joanna was watching again, her hand on my arm, squinting into the sunlight, her eyes following the police car as it slowly headed out into the shimmer of the causeway, her face once more betraying no emotion.

Behind us, Bannion pulled up in his Range Rover and sat surveying the crowd, frowning. I ignored him. I stood with Joanna, eyes crinkled against the sun, watching the police car turn into a shimmering dot on the horizon. A couple of policemen were conferring over whatever it was that Jack had given them. One of them crossed to where we stood.

"He wanted you to have this," he said to Joanna, "but I'm afraid it's evidence." She said nothing, looking at what he had in his hand. It looked like some kind of a tin.

"It's Uluru," she said finally, and burst into tears.

Suddenly everyone spoke at once, the little gaggle of people broke up into smaller groups, talking and giving opinions. I could see Billy among them, self-important with his version of events. They would all have plenty to say in the bar of the Red Lion tonight. Cath came and put an uncertain arm around her weeping daughter.

"We'll go back to London together," she said. "We'll start again. You, me and Gaby. As soon as we've got the rape business out of the way."

Joanna was shaking her head, decisive through her tears. I realised I had never seen her cry before. "There wasn't a rape," she said loudly, making sure everyone could hear. "I'm not pressing charges." She moved away, a small, quick movement, freeing herself from her mother and heading towards me, sniffing and wiping her face on her sleeve.

"Come on, hen," I said quietly. "You must be starving."

I began to walk away with her, but then she suddenly stooped down. In a sudden movement that was too unexpected to prevent, she had scooped up a rock and hurled it straight at Billy. He ducked, and the thing whistled past his ear, and then I heard the crash of broken glass and realised I had been mistaken: the rock had not been meant for Billy, who was sitting on the damp shingle, shocked, sand in his trouser turn-ups. Behind him, Bannion sat shouting and hysterical behind the smashed window of his Range Rover with the Verbena Hotel logo on the side.

A muted cheer rose up from the islanders. Joanna grinned at me. I grinned back. "Politics in your veins," I said. "Blood will out."

* * *

They took me and Joanna and Cath back home in a squad car, and then it was a long time before they all left. Joanna would have to report to the station at Berwick tomorrow and they told us to get a solicitor. I had to shut the dog upstairs, it was so excited by all the people.

After they had gone, we sat in the kitchen, Joanna hanging over the range to get warm, me spooning tea from the caddy into the pot for the umpteenth time, Cath smoking and pouring herself a drink, even though it was eleven o'clock in the morning.

"I'll make pan haggerty for our dinner," I told Joanna. She liked pan haggerty.

"Without meat?" Cath asked hopefully. I ignored her. She inhaled on her cigarette and glowered at me spitefully. "A few more days and you'll be back in McDonald's, eh, Joanna? Thought I didn't know. I saw you in there. School lunch-times. The one on Seven Sisters Road."

Joanna stared into space, her cold little hands caressing the warm rail where I hung the tea towels. She was thinking about Jack Dalton, I expect.

Cath turned again to me. "Would you mind keeping the dog? I really don't think it's kind to keep a dog in a flat, and anyway, we haven't got time to exercise it."

I started to pull potatoes out of the box in the pantry. Nice big pink-skinned King Edwards I dug up before all this ballyhoo started. Cath was still talking, but I wasn't really listening. I selected the biggest and dropped them into my apron, then took them to the sink for peeling.

"Term will be starting in a couple of weeks . . . you need some new shoes . . . sort out the curriculum for my Late Readers . . . Gaby says he's missing us –"

Joanna let out a strange little yelp, half-laughter, half-anger. She came and stood next to me at the sink, and picked up the potato peeler. "Can I stay here?" she asked me.

I didn't have time to even consider my answer, because Cath interrupted. "Don't be silly, Joanna. You've got school."

"I'm not going." Joanna was peeling a large potato quickly and badly.

I took the potato out of her hand. "Here, Miss Cackhands. Like this."

Cath sighed impatiently. "Look, I know you're angry with me. I was angry with you, all right? So we're quits. Only I think we've got to try again, Joanna. Make this work. You're my daughter." Joanna watched my demonstration for a moment, then nodded, distracted, retrieved the potato and continued to peel it as badly as before. "We can't stay here, Jo. It's running away. We should never have come." *Thanks very much*, I thought. Joanna said nothing, but she was certainly listening. "I've spoken to your dad, and he says let's all make a new start –"

Joanna slammed down the peeler and the potato plopped into the bowl. "You spoke to him?" She wouldn't look at her mother, I noticed. I could almost see her heart banging away.

"I phoned him," Cath said. "I had to tell him you'd been attacked and that you'd run away. You might have gone back to him, for all I knew."

Joanna snorted. "You must be joking." She retrieved the potato, and would have peeled it all over again if I hadn't taken it from her and given her another one. She set about it with ferocity.

Cath slammed her hand down on the table. "I'm trying, Joanna," she said finally in a sharp voice. "I've got a daughter who thinks she's Lolita, but I'm trying."

"That's not fair," I said, surprised by the sound of my own utterance.

"Yes. Well. Life isn't fair," Cath said. Joanna was going through the potatoes like a dose of salts. All I could do was watch. "I'm prepared to put the incident in London behind us –"

"Incident!" Joanna exploded.

"Yes. And the rape accusation that came to nothing, and the running away and spending the night with a man old enough to be your father –"

That was it. Joanna turned, the peeler held up like a dagger, and I grabbed her and snatched it away, pushing her hard against the sink. She began to cry, furious tears. "Don't speak about him in the same breath as Gaby," she said.

"He wants us back. He sent you his love." Now Cath was crying too, her chin wobbling, her face streaked with red.

"I don't want his love. Not the kind he wants to give me," Joanna said in a very small voice. I looked at her. She had turned back to the sink and was holding her hands in the muddy water, turning a potato over and over in her palm.

"What are you saying?" I asked her. She shook her head.

"She's not saying anything," Cath said. "She thinks she's got a starring role in some John Hughes film. Molly bloody Ringwald. Everything's a drama, isn't it, Joanna? Everything's over the top."

Joanna didn't raise her head. But she spoke, in that

same low voice. "Me and him. You know what we did. He started it."

"I don't want to hear your nasty little accusations."

Joanna began to shout, then. "He hurt me! I was nine years old! I was nine, Mum. I was nine!"

I'd like to think that when I heard her say it, I immediately knew that what she was saying was true, and that the scales fell from my eyes and everything changed from that moment. But I might be glossing over things with time. All I really remember about that moment is the air quivering between these two, my daughter and her daughter, and those words hanging in the silence. Then Cath spoke.

"I don't believe you," she said.

"Cathy –"

She started yelling then, at me. "Shut up! Always sticking your oar in – you've turned her head, you and that American, listening to her spiteful little lies, believing her stories, all spewing out of that nasty evil little teenage brain, fed on crap magazines and crap telly and crap friends and crap newspapers and cheap horrible sensational hysterical scandal . . . " She was blubbing, distraught, ranting. "Foul, ugly, loathsome little brain making up lies, any lies, so that the world will sit up and look at her and take notice, so that she's interesting and people listen. You and that Yank, you did this to her, encouraging her, egging her on – and *you* –" she stabbed a finger in my direction – "*you* let him come into the house, you let him sit in here and drink your tea, a criminal, a murderer –"

"He isn't!" Joanna was crying now. I could feel her trembling next to me. "He isn't a murderer – he's Scott Walker. From the Walker Brothers. Scott Walker."

"Like hell he is. He bloody told me, Joanna. He told me what he is. A maker of bombs, a blower-up of human beings, a killer of innocent people, he's like the IRA, he's like the Serbs, he's like the Russians in Chechnya –"

"No."

"Yes. The man is a fugitive from justice. And he most certainly is not Scott Walker. You think I wouldn't know if Scott Walker walked in the room? You stupid, stupid girl."

Joanna's tears had been dashed away by a wet, grubby hand. She was standing upright, head erect, as I always thought of her, in that aggressive, proud way she had when roused. "You're wrong."

Cath shook her head. "I'm not. Jack Dalton never was and never will be Scott Walker."

Joanna gave a small, derisive laugh that turned into a choking noise. "Yes," she said. "He is." – and began stacking the peeled potatoes onto the draining board.

Stalemate.

I decided to step in. "So," I said dryly, "seems like you're quits, Cath, like you said. You don't believe Joanna, and she doesn't believe you."

"And what about you, Mam? Who do you believe?"

I didn't know what to say. I had one of those bleak little yearning moments when you wish everything could just go back and be the way it was: life with a steady pattern to it, complicated but manageable, like the Aran jumper. "Shall I do green beans with this?" I asked. Cath stood up and pushed her chair back.

"Thanks very much," she said, her voice uneven. "Thanks a bunch, Mother."

She only ever called me mother when she was angry. She left the room, slamming the door. Upstairs the dog barked, surprised by the noise. Joanna pulled a pan from its hook and began to fill it with water. I headed for the back door. It wouldn't take me many minutes to pick the beans.

* * *

I stand in the road and signal to Billy to stop. I see his eyes light up, but I don't respond. He opens the door and looks at me, his expression intense, rather foolish. I've lent Cath my old suitcase, pulled down from the top of the wardrobe. It's the same one I took to London when I went to try and persuade her not to give up being a student. It seems right that it should go back there, with her. There are no goodbyes. Joanna stands silently next to me, her expression the one she usually has – closed-off, secret. I look along the bus windows. Eyes slide away from mine, not knowing how to react after everything that's happened. I don't mind. They'll forget. It will all go back to being the way it was. There will be a funeral for that boy and his mother will weep and curse Jack Dalton, believing that he killed her son; but it will happen somewhere else, Morpeth I suppose – not here, not on Holy Island. Here, winter will come, the hills will be covered in snow, the tourists will have disappeared, and we'll all go back to doing what we always do, and waiting for another summer. The only difference will be that Jack Dalton will have gone, and Joanna will be here.

Billy is leaning out of his driver's seat. "Shall I come by after my shift?" he asks.

I shake my head. "I've got chutney to make."

The doors wheeze shut and the bus sets off. No farewells, no kisses, no hugs. I can see Cath making her way to the back of the bus as it lurches off. Joanna has already gone back into the house. I watch the bus disappear round the corner, on its way to Chare Ends. I wonder if Cath will look back from the causeway, for a last glimpse of the glittering sea, the dark hulk of the castle on the hill, the cottages clustered round the harbour, before the mists fold in and it all disappears forever. "Like *Brigadoon* . . . " She would say.

I go inside. The dog is waiting on the threshold. This morning it tried to creep into Joanna's room and I heard her say "Piss off" – but not in an angry way. A few more days and she won't even notice it's there.

I go into the kitchen and start sorting out the pans for the chutney. I've made a deal with my granddaughter: I won't make her go back to London if she'll agree to go to school. I'm going to sort her out a place at Alnwick Girls', they've got a minibus that will pick her up and drop her off; and when the tide's in and she can't get back to the island she can sleep in the back bedroom at Davy Redpath's sister's house on Bondgate. I've asked him already, and he's getting on the phone to his sister tonight.

It's my chance, you see, to make everything all right.

I start chopping tomatoes. A deep, dark voice floats down from Joanna's lair. Scott Walker is singing. I listen while I work. The music solidifies, takes on shape.

Joanna . . .

I can't forget the one they call Joanna . . .

I've got plenty of flour and currants. If Billy calls later, the three of us can have Singing Hinnies for tea.

THE END